> *"How many Sacketts are there?"*
> *"Nobody rightly knows, but even one Sackett*
> *is quite a few."*

Being hunted by men who want you dead is no way to live.

Especially when you're heading through unfamiliar territory like the wild Big Sandy River country leading two pilgrims who are supposed to be protecting *you*.

So, Echo Sackett was just a wee bit concerned about her situation. Sure, she had not missed a shot with her hunting rifle since last August—and then it had only been a case of her target disappearing before her bullet hit the mark. However, Echo had never been in a real shootin' *fight* before.

There was always the chance that some of the fierce Clinch Mountain Sackett cousins like Mordecai, the long hunter, Trulove, or Macon would come running when there was trouble. But true to her Sackett blood, Echo was not about to wait to be rescued. She knew it was time for the hunted to fight back:

> *"We've got to cut them down, make them*
> *understand there's a price to pay."*

Bantam Books by Louis L'Amour
Ask your bookseller for the books you have missed

# RIDE
# THE RIVER
## LOUIS L'AMOUR

BANTAM BOOKS

TORONTO • NEW YORK • LONDON • SYDNEY • AUCKLAND

RIDE THE RIVER
*A Bantam Book / July 1983*

2nd printing ..... July 1983     4th printing ... October 1983
3rd printing ..... July 1983     5th printing ..... June 1984
6th printing ..... April 1985

**ISBN 0-553-25274-7**

*Published simultaneously in the United States and Canada*

PRINTED IN THE UNITED STATES OF AMERICA

**H**    15 14 13 12 11 10

To Norman Millen

# 1

When daylight crested Siler's Bald, I taken up my carpetbag and rifle and followed the Middle Prong toward Tuckalucky Cove.

"Echo," Ma said, "if you be goin' to the Settlements you better lay down that rifle-gun an' set up a few nights with a needle.

"You take them *Godey's Lady's Books* the pack-peddler left with us and give them study. City folks dress a sight different than we-uns and you don't want to shame yourself."

There was money coming to us and I was to go fetch it home. Pa had wore hisself out scratchin' a livin' from a side-hill farm, and a few months back he give up the fight and "went west," as the sayin' was. We buried him yonder where the big oak stands and marked his place with letterin' on a stone.

The boys were trappin' beaver in the Shining Mountains far to the westward and there was nobody t' home but Regal an' me, and Regal was laid up. He'd had a mite of a set-to with a cross bear who didn't recognize him for a Sackett. There'd been a sight of jawin' an' clawin' before Regal stretched him out, Regal usin' what he had to hand, a knife and a double-bit ax. Trouble was Regal got himself chawed and clawed in the doin' of it and was in no shape for travel.

Me, I'd been huntin' meat for the table since I was shorter than the rifle I carried and the last few years I'd killed so much I was sellin' meat to the butcher. No sooner did I get a mite of money more'n what was needed than I began dreamin' over the fancy fixin's in Godey's fashion magazine.

When a girl gets to be sixteen, it's time she set her cap for a man but I'd yet to see one for whom I'd fetch an' carry. Like any girl, I'd done a sight of dreamin', but not about the boys along Fightin' Creek or the Middle Prong. My dreams were of somethin' far off an' fancy. Part of that was due to Regal.

Regal was my uncle, a brother to Pa, and when he was a boy he'd gone off a-yonderin' along the mountains to the Settlements. We had kinfolk down to Charleston and he visited there before continuing on his way. He told me of folks he met there, of their clothes, the homes they lived in, the theayters they went to an' the fancy food.

Regal had been out among 'em in his time an' I suspect he'd cut some fancy didoes wherever he went. Regal was tall, stronger than three bulls, and quick with a smile that made a girl tingle to her toes. Many of them told me that very thing, and although many a girl set her cap for Regal, he was sly to all their ways and wary of traps. Oh, he had a way with him, Regal did!

"Don't you be in no hurry," he advised me. "You're cute as a button and you've got a nice shape. You're enough to start any man a-wonderin' where his summer wages went.

"You hold your horses. No need to marry up with somebody just because the other girls are doin' it. I've been yonder where folks live different and there's a better way than to spend your years churnin' milk an' hoeing corn. But one word of caution: don't you be lettin' the boys know how good you can shoot. Not many men would like to be bested by a spit of a girl not five feet tall!"

"I'm five-feet-two!" I protested.

"You mind what I say. When you get down to the Settlements, you mind your P's an' Q's. When a man talks to a girl, he's not as honest as he might be, although at the time he half-believes it all himself. There's times a man will promise a girl anything an' forget his promises before the hour's up."

"Did you make promises like that, Regal?"

"No, I never. When a woman sees a man she wants, there's no need to promise or even say very much. A woman will come up with better answers than any poor mountain boy could think up. I was kind of shy there at first, then I found it was workin' for me so I just kept on bein' shy.

"Womenfolks have powerful imaginations when it comes to a man, an' she can read things into him he never knew was there, and like as not, they ain't!"

Turning to look back, I could still see Blanket and Thunderhead Mountains and the end of Davis Ridge. It was clouding up and coming on to rain.


Philadelphia had more folks in it than I reckoned there was in the world. When I stepped down from the stage I made query of the driver as to where I was wishful of goin' and he stepped out into the street and pointed the way.

The place I was heading for was a rooming-and-boarding house kept by a woman who had kinfolk in the mountains. It was reckoned a safe place for a young girl to stay. Not that I was much worried. I had me an Arkansas toothpick slung in its scabbard inside my dress and a little slit pocket where I could reach through the folds to fetch it. In my carpetbag I carried a pistol.

Most unmarried folks and others who were married ate in boardinghouses, them days. Restaurants were for folks with money or for an evening on the town. Folks who worked in shops and the like hunted places where there was room an' board, although some roomed in one place and boarded elsewhere.

Amy Sulky had twelve rooms to let but she set table for twenty-four. She had two setups for breakfast, one for noontime, as most carried lunches to their work or caught a snack nearby or from a street vendor. At suppertime she had two settin's again.

I'd writ Amy so she knew I was comin' and had kept a place for me. A nice room it was, too, mighty luxurious for the likes of me, with curtains to the windows, a rag rug on the floor, a bed, a chair, and a washstand with a white china bowl and pitcher on it.

First thing when I got to my room was take a peek past the curtain, and sure enough, the man who followed me from the stage was outside, makin' like he was readin' a newspaper.

When a girl grows up in Injun country hunting all her born days, she becomes watchful. Gettin' down from the stage, I saw that man see me like I was somebody expected. Making a point of not seemin' to notice, I started off up the street, but when I stopped at a crossing, I noticed him fold his newspaper and start after me.

Back in the high country folks said I was a right pretty girl, but that cut no figure here. Any girl knows when a man notices her because she's pretty, but this man had no such ideas in mind. I'd hunted too much game not to know when I am hunted myself.

If he wasn't followin' because he liked my looks, then why? Anybody could see I wasn't well-off. My clothes were pretty because I'd made them myself, but they weren't fancy city clothes. As I didn't look to be carryin' money, why should he follow me?

My reason for coming to Philadelphia was to meet up with a lawyer and collect money that was due me. By all accounts it was a goodly sum, but who could know that?

Somebody might have talked too much. The lawyer himself or his clerk, if he had such a thing. Most folks like to talk and seem important. Given special knowledge, they can't wait to speak of it.

The only reason I could think of for someone to follow me was because he knew what I'd come for and meant to have it.

Back yonder, folks warned of traps laid for young girls in the cities, but none of that worried me. I was coming to get money, and once I had it in hand, I was going right back where I came from. In my short years I'd had some going round and about with varmints, and although I hadn't my rifle with me, I did have a pistol and my Arkansas toothpick. It was two-edged, razor-sharp, with a point like a needle. If a body so much as fell against that point, it would go in to the hilt, it was that sharp.

Amy Sulky set a good table. She seated me on her left and told folks I was a friend from Tennessee. The city folks at the table bowed, smiled, and said their howdy-dos.

There was a tall, straight woman with her hair parted down the middle who looked like she'd been weaned on a sour pickle, and there was a plump gentleman with muttonchop whiskers who gave me the merest nod and went back to serious eating. Seemed to me he figured he'd paid for his board and was going to be sure he got his money's worth, and maybe his neighbor's, too. Opposite me sat a quiet, serious-looking man with a bald head and a pointed beard. He was neat, attractive, and friendly. He asked if I intended to stay in the city and I told him I was leaving as soon as I'd done what I came for.

One thing led to another and I told him about us seeing that item about property left to the "youngest descendant of Kin Sackett." I told him we'd found the notice in the *Penny Advocate*. It had come wrapped around some goods sold us by the pack peddler.

"That strikes me as odd, Mrs. Sulky," he said, turning to her. "The *Advocate* has but a small circulation here in Pennsylvania. I imagine few copies get beyond the borders of the state. It must have been sheer chance that Miss Sackett saw the item at all."

He glanced at me. "Have you inquired at the address?"

"No, sir, I have just come to town. We wrote to them and they said I must come to Philadelphia to establish my relationship."

"Odd," he said again. "It is none of my business, of course, but the procedure seems peculiar. I know nothing of the legalities. Perhaps they were required to advertise for heirs, but if so, they used an unlikely method. No doubt they were surprised when they heard from you."

The talk turned to other things, but he'd put a bee in my bonnet. I said nothing about being followed, as more than likely they would think it was my imagination, but more and more I was wondering if there mightn't be some crookedness afoot. If any money was coming to us, we wanted it and our family hadn't had any cash money to speak of for longer than I wished to remember.

It was a puzzler that we'd been left money by kinfolk of Kin Sackett, because Kin had been dead for nigh onto two hundred years.

Kin was the first of our blood born on American soil. His pappy had been old Barnabas Sackett, who settled on Shooting Creek, in North Carolina. He and some of his ship's crew had done well, finding some gem sapphires east of where Barnabas settled.

Barnabas was killed by Injuns near what was called Crab Orchard, and Kin became the old man of the family. His younger brother Yance settled in the Clinch

Mountains, where he raised a brood of wild boys who would fight at the drop of a hat and drop it themselves. Those boys grew up back at the forks of the creek and were raised on bear meat and sourwood honey, but now I was the youngest of Kin's line.

At breakfast Amy Sulky advised me to have a care. "This town is full of sharpers trying to take money from honest folk."

"I've no money for bait," I said. "When I pay you, and my fare on the stage, I'll have nothing left but eating money. The little I have was earned a-hunting."

"Hunting?" The fat man stared at me.

"Yes, sir. My brothers went west, so if there was meat on the table it was up to me. We ate real good, but I shot so much I commenced selling to the butcher."

"Powder and ball cost money!"

"Yes, sir, but I don't miss very often. Nor do I shoot unless my chances are good."

"Even so, one does miss."

"Yes, sir. I missed one time last August. Mistook a stub of a branch for a squirrel. That squirrel ducked from sight and I seen that stub of branch. I hit what I shot at, but it was no squirrel."

"You mean to say you haven't missed a shot since last August?"

"You come from the mountains, Mrs. Sulky. You can tell him how folks are about wastin' powder an' shot. Pappy taught us to hit what we shot at. Mostly we do, and that includes Regal."

"Ah, that Regal!" Amy Sulky said wistfully. "Did he ever marry?"

"Not so's you'd notice. He says he will when the right girl comes along."

When I started to leave the house, the man with the bald head was leaving too. "Miss Sackett? I know nothing of your affairs, but be careful. Don't offer any information you don't have to, and above all, don't sign any papers."

"Yes, sir, thank you, sir."

The man with the newspaper was standing near a rig tied across the street. He was a thickset man wearing a gray hard hat and a houndstooth coat. If he was wishful of not being seen, he was a stupid man. I walked away up the street, and after a moment, he followed.

# 2

James White had an office on a small avenue that ran into Broad Street. The nice gentleman with the bald head and beard had directed me.

On this day I carried a knitting bag and I had some knitting in it. I also had my pistol. The Arkansas toothpick was in its usual place and ready to hand.

Womenfolks did not go armed in Philadelphia, Ma said, unless they carried a hatpin, but nobody needed hatpins with the poke bonnets everybody was wearing. I let mine sort of hang back on my neck by its ribbon because I could see better from the corners of my eyes, and I'd spent too much time in the woods to want my vision blocked to the sides.

There were handsome buildings to right and left, with marble steps. The streets were of brick. Passing by a building with a beautiful marble front to it and marble steps, all the marble with blue veins, I glimpsed some brass plates with the names of the occupants on them.

One I noticed in particular because it had a familiar sound.

### CHANTRY & CHANTRY, LAWYERS

Seemed to me it was a name I'd heard at storytelling time back in the mountains. We'd set around with the fire crackling, sometimes popping corn or having a taffy pull, and there would be stories told.

Sure enough, I found James White's office on a side street. Opening the door, I entered and found it was a small room with a couple of hard chairs, a sofa, and a small desk with a young man settin' behind it. Yet just as I entered, the door across the room was closing and I caught a glimpse of a boot heel and some pants leg before the door closed. Looked like that man who followed me, but how he could have gotten ahead without me seeing him, I did not know. Maybe it was somebody else.

The young man behind the desk had rumpled hair and a sly look to him. He looked kind of unwashed and slept-in. He looked at me impudent-like and said, "What's for you?"

"I would like to see Mr. White. Tell him Miss Sackett is here."

He sat there for a minute like he had no idea of moving, and then he stood up. "Sackett, is it? You that hillbilly girl?"

"If you will tell Mr. White that I am here. . . ."

"Little thing, ain't you?"

"I am as big as I need to be."

He leered. "Reckon that's so. Yes, sir! I reckon you're right, at that!"

"Mr. White, please."

He turned lazily and went to the door, opened it, and said, "Girl to see you. Name of Sackett."

There was the sound of a chair moving and then the young man drew back and an older man, short and heavyset, pushed by him. His black hair was slicked down over a round skull. As he came through the door he was shrugging into a coat, and he wore a bushy mustache.

His wide smile revealed more teeth than I'd seen in a long time and he said, "Miss Sackett? I am James White. Will you come in, please?"

He let me go past him and then he followed, waving me to a chair and sitting down behind his desk. "Is this your first trip to Philadelphia, Miss Sackett?"

"Yes, sir. We don't have much occasion to come down to the Settlements."

"Settlements?" He looked surprised, then chuckled. "Of course! Settlements. I suspect it has been a long time since Philadelphia has been referred to as a Settlement."

"I came about the money."

"Ah, yes. Of course. You can prove who you are, Miss Sackett? I mean, that you are a descendant of Kin Sackett?"

"I can."

"A considerable sum is involved. Of course, there will be charges against it. My fees, the advertising. . . ."

He waved a hand, smiling and showing all those teeth. "But what am I doing? Talking business with a lovely young lady on her first trip to Philadelphia! We should be planning to go out upon the town! Business can come later."

"I'd as soon tend to it now. I don't aim . . . I mean, I don't intend to stay longer than necessary. I'd like to get this over with."

"Of course you would! But I cannot be lacking in hospitality! You must let me take you to one of our restaurants, where we can discuss business at leisure."

"No."

Startled, White stared at me with cold eyes. "You refuse? I assure you—"

"Not to be impolite, sir, but I think we should discuss business first. I must return to the mountains. If you will just tell me how much is coming to me and what remains to be done, we can get along with it."

White was irritated, and he concealed it poorly. What he had in mind, I had no idea, but obviously getting down to business was not part of it.

Why was he delaying? Did he really intend to be hospitable? Or did he hope to turn my head with entertainment and the glitter of the city? Although I was yet to see much glitter in Philadelphia. It looked to me like a get-down-to-business place, as befitted the greatest city in the land. There was much I wished to see had there been time, but there was work to be done back home.

Was the money here? Had he, as my friend at Mrs. Sulky's suggested, deliberately advertised in an unlikely publication?

James White leaned back in his chair and his eyes reminded me of something . . . Of a weasel. "You say your name is Sackett and you are from Tennessee?"

"You know my name. I wrote to you from Tennessee."

He seemed to be hesitating, trying to figure which trail to take. If he intended to pay me the money, he had only to make sure who I was and hand it over. I would sign for it, of course. It struck me as a straightforward proposition.

If he planned to steal the money, somehow something had thrown his plans out of kilter. Maybe he had not expected anybody to see his advertisement or answer it. Or maybe he had figured a sixteen-year-old mountain girl would be easy to deal with. Whatever, he figured something had gone wrong for him or was going wrong.

"How did you happen to see the item in the *Advocate*?"

"It came wrapped around some goods we bought from the pack peddler." For the first time an idea occurred to me. "Fact is, I believe the peddler saw that notice and wrapped it around the goods a-purpose."

"Why would he do that?"

"So's we could read it. Mountain folks read everything that comes to hand. It ain't much—*isn't* much, I should say. He would know that and he would know the item concerned our kinfolk."

"Who is this peddler you speak of?"

"Never did know his name. I doubt if anybody knows, or where he comes from or how old he is. He peddles goods in the mountains and he tinkers with things, fixes guns, clocks, and the like, although nobody has much use for a clock except as something to listen to when you're alone."

"How do you tell time?"

"We know when it's daylight and we know when it's dark. What else would be needed?"

"What about appointments?"

"You mean meetin' somebody? If I am wishful to see somebody, I go to his house or the field where he's workin'. He does the same if he wishes to see me. Or we can meet at church of a Sunday."

"And if he doesn't go to church?"

"In the mountains? Everybody goes to church. Even George Haliday . . . he's our atheist. We go to meet folks as well as to hear the preachin' an' singin'. George, he goes so he can hear what the preacher says so's they can argue about it at the store."

"They are friends?"

"Of course. Everybody likes George, and the preacher looks forward to those arguments. Ever'body down to the store does. They argued about the whale swallowin' Jonah until the preacher came up with evidence showin' two men had been swallowed and lived to tell of it.

"Preacher, he says for all his mistaken ways George knows more Bible than anybody he ever knew. He says that down inside, George Haliday is a good Christian man who just likes to argue. I wouldn't know about that, but ever' once in a while the preacher throws a sermon right at him, and all the folks know it and they watch George."

"The tinker who brought the *Advocate?* Do you see him often?"

"Ever' two, three months. Sometimes oftener. He comes down along the ridge trail carryin' a pack so big you'd think it would take three men. Packs it all by hisself."

"Doesn't he ever get robbed?"

Well, I just looked at him. Where was he raised? Nobody would rob a pack peddler, but especially not this one. Anyway, even among Injuns, peddlers an' traders were respected an' let be. We all needed their goods. If the peddler stopped comin', we'd all lack for things.

"Nobody would rob the Tinker. I reckon nobody could. He's got him a special kind of knife he makes himself, and knows how to use it. I often wished I had one like it, but I have to make do with my pick."

" 'Pick'?"

"Arkansas toothpick." When I said it, I could see he was ignorant. "It's a kind of knife."

He stared at me there for a moment, tryin' to make me out. I reckon I was a different kind of person than he'd ever met. So I changed the subject on him.

"About that money. Folks where I come from, Mr. White, are right serious about money. When somebody owes money, they pay it or explain why they can't. You have money for me. I want it."

"Of course. You are impatient, but I understand that." He reached in his desk and drew out a paper with all kinds of writin' on it and indicated a line at the bottom. "You just sign right there and you shall have your money."

Me, I just looked at him. "Mr. White, I don't figure to sign anything until I have the money in hand. All of it. You put the money on the desk and I'll sign fast enough."

"I am sorry, Miss Sackett. Your signing would expedite matters. In any event, it shall have to be tomorrow, as I naturally would not have such a sum in my office."

I stood up. "Yes, sir. I understand, sir. Tomorrow morning I will be here and you had better be, with that money. If it ain't here or you aren't, I'll start backtrackin' that money. I reckon any kind of money leaves its trail, and I can read sign as good as anybody. I'll follow that trail right back to where it come from an' right back to you, so's I will know how much is involved an' why you keep putting me off."

He stood up too. "There's nothing to worry about, Miss Sackett. Your money will be here. However"—and there was a hard edge to his voice—"I would advise you to change your tone. You are in Philadelphia now, Miss Sackett, not back in your mountains. You would do well to curb your tongue."

"You have that money for me and you'll not have to put up with me."

He started to speak angrily, then changed his mind. He changed it so fast the words backed up on him, but he finally come out with it. "I am sorry, Miss Sackett, we seem to have gotten off on the wrong foot. I did not wish to offend you or cause unnecessary delays. I only hoped to make your stay more agreeable."

To be honest, that was all he had done. Maybe I'd been set on edge by the doubts of my bald-headed friend or something in James White's manner, or the fact that I'd been followed from the time I arrived in town. Come to think on it, he'd said nothing a body could take offense to.

"I am sorry too," I said. "I shall be here in the morning."

# 3

When I fetched myself to the sidewalk, the tall young man from the office was standin' there. He looked me up and down, impudent as you please, and then he said, "Come along, Miss Sackett, and I'll walk you home."

"No, thanks. I shall walk by myself. I have much to do."

He laughed at me, not a very nice laugh. "How'd you an' ol' White get along? You better watch him. He's got an eye for the girls."

I walked across the street, and was so irritated that I did not notice whether I was followed or not. It was several blocks before I thought to look, but I saw nobody. It was late afternoon and folks had either gone home or were going.

Turning back, I saw I was in front of the building with the brass nameplates, and there it was again: "CHANTRY & CHANTRY, LAWYERS."

Up the steps I went and into a hall where several

doors had names on them. Opening the Chantry door, I
stepped into an outer office that was all shadowed and
still. There were two desks and chairs, and along one
side was a leather settee for those who waited. The
door to an inner office was open a crack and I could
hear the scratching of a pen. Stepping into the door, I
peered inside.

A white-haired man was sitting behind a desk, writing.
Piled beside him were several lawbooks, and one of
them was open.

As I peeked in, he looked up, right into my eyes. He
stared at me as if not believing what he saw, and I
stared back, embarrassed.

He stood up, and he was very tall. Tall as Regal,
maybe, but not so muscular. "Will you come in, please?
My clerk has gone home, I believe." He came around
the desk. "I am Finian Chantry."

Taking a further step into the room, I stood, my feet
together, very erect, very prim. "I am Echo Sackett."

He gestured to a chair, then turned back to his desk,
pausing in mid-stride. "Sackett, did you say? *Sackett?*"

"Yes, sir. I am afraid I am presuming, sir, but there
was no one in the outer office and I hoped to have a
word with you, sir."

"Sit down, Miss Sackett. Echo, did you say? What a
pretty name!"

"I am glad you think so, sir. Many think it strange,
but we live in the mountains, sir, and my father loved
the echoes."

"The mountains? Tennessee, no doubt?"

"Why, yes, sir. How did you know? Oh! My accent!"

"On the contrary, Miss Sackett. I once knew someone of your name, a very long time ago, and he was
from Tennessee."

Finian Chantry moved some papers aside, and mark-
ing his place in the open book, closed it. "He was a fine
man, a great man in his way. Were it not for him, I

might not be here tonight. He was a good friend to me, and an older friend of my brother's."

"If you could tell me his name, sir?"

"Daubeny Sackett. He fought in the Battle of King's Mountain, among others."

"He was my grandfather, sir."

Finian Chantry sat back in his chair. With his shock of white hair and his lean, strong features, he was a strikingly handsome man.

"Then perhaps I can call you Echo?" His face became serious. "Now, Echo, what can I do for you?"

Seated across from him, I told him my story as simply and directly as possible. How we had seen the notice in the *Penny Advocate* and how I had written to James White and had come to claim my inheritance.

"This inheritance. Do you know from whom it comes?"

"No, sir. It was to go to the youngest of Kin Sackett's line, so whoever left the money must have known our family for a very long time. Kin Sackett has been dead for two hundred years."

"Strange," Chantry agreed, "but interesting, very interesting. And this James White advertised in the *Penny Advocate*?"

"Yes, sir, and anyone who knew of Kin Sackett would know we lived in Tennessee or west of there."

He got to his feet. "Miss Sackett, I shall escort you home. It is not well for a young girl to be on the streets of Philadelphia at night, even if she is a Sackett."

When we went outside, a carriage pulled up before the door and a man stepped down to open the door for us. Riding in a carriage! If only Ma could see me now!

"Tomorrow when you call upon Mr. White, I shall attend you. I scarcely believe there will be trouble."


James White sat at his desk staring at the accumulated papers, a disgusted expression on his face. He glanced up as the thickset man in the square gray hat entered.

"What is it, Tim? I am busy!"

"You'll be busier if you expect to pull this off. You take my advice an' get to that hillbilly girl an' get her to sign a release."

"When did I ask your advice?"

"You never did. That ain't to say you couldn't have used it a time or two. That hillbilly girl's no damn fool. She's gone to another lawyer."

"*What?* Who?"

"She went right from here to Chantry's office. Walked right in."

"That's impossible!"

"You believe that an' you're liable to find yourself in jail. Old Chantry's nobody to fool with. You know it an' I know it."

White brushed his mustache with a forefinger, throwing a quick, angry look at Tim Oats. Inwardly he was cursing. It had all looked so simple! Everybody on the O'Hara side was dead, the money was in his hands, and Brunn's widow trusted him implicitly. He had made an attempt to find the heirs that would pass muster with her, and he could do what he wished with the money until he found the heirs, which he had hoped never to do. Who would dream a copy of that little sheet would ever find its way into the backwoods of Tennessee?

"Chantry doesn't handle such cases," White said impatiently. "His practice is in admiralty law or international trade. Anyway, how could a hillbilly girl even get his attention?"

"All I know is that she left here and went right to his office. She opened the door and walked right in."

"And probably came right out."

"I figured I'd best get to you. Chantry is tough, an' you know how he feels about the law. To him it's a sacred trust, an' if he finds you playin' fast an' loose, he'll put you behind bars."

"You don't have to explain Finian Chantry to me. I know all about him."

James White was irritated and a little frightened. Still, he had done nothing wrong . . . yet. He touched his tongue to dry lips. Thank God he had been warned. Grudgingly he glanced at Tim Oats. "Thanks. You did the right thing, coming right to me."

Finian Chantry had fought in the Revolution. He had been an important government official at the time of the War of 1812. It was said he had refused a seat on the Supreme Court for reasons of health. He was a man accustomed to power and the use of power.

Tim Oats was right. He should have smoothed things over and gotten the Sackett girl to sign a release. He could have given her a few dollars. . . . After all, the girl had no idea what was involved.

Of course, that was what he had planned. To take her to a plush restaurant, give her a couple of glasses of wine, then produce some gold money and get her to sign a release as "paid in full." Then she turned him down.

Turned *him* down! Who did she think she was, anyway?

Yet slowly caution began to slip through the cracks in his ego. Chantry, he was sure, would not give her the time of day, but the sooner the Sackett girl was back in her mountains, the better.

When old Adam Brunn died suddenly, his widow had asked White to settle her husband's legal affairs. The old man had a small but solid practice, mostly with estates and land titles, but White agreed immediately. Had the widow known anyone else, she would not have asked him, but a friend of White's had been helping her through the trying period after her husband's death, and had recommended White.

Most of what Brunn had left unfinished was routine and offered no chance for chicanery. Then he had come upon the O'Hara papers.

Apparently, many years before, one Kane O'Hara had been an associate of Barnabas Sackett, whoever he was, and later, of his son, Kin Sackett. Partly due to the Sackett association, Kane O'Hara had done well financially, leaving a considerable estate to his heirs. In his will he left a provision that if at any time the O'Hara family was left without an heir in the immediate line, what remained of the estate should go to the youngest living descendant of Kin Sackett.

To White it seemed a foolish document, but all of the subsequent heirs had included the provision in their wills as well, and for a while there had been some association with the Sackett family. At last the event had taken place, and a search for the youngest Sackett had begun.

Adam Brunn's conscientious search for the heirs discovered the Sackett family living in Tennessee, and Brunn had drawn up an advertisement to appear in some Tennessee newspapers just before he died. His widow was determined Brunn's wishes be carried out, as apparently this was one facet of his business he had discussed with her. White proceeded to advertise, but deliberately chose a paper unlikely to be found in Tennessee.

The letter from Echo Sackett had come as a shock, for he was already devising ways by which the money could remain in his hands. White's income varied between six and seven hundred dollars per year, a goodly sum in 1840. The inheritance came to something more than three thousand dollars, and in addition, there was a small iron cube, a puzzle box of some sort, composed of many movable parts, each one a small square with its own symbol or hieroglyphic.

That iron box or cube or whatever it was had become an irritation to White. It must have some significance, for it was mentioned in the will and was obviously important. He had worked over it, turning the various bits and pieces. Some of the squares slid from place to place and could be realigned to make different combinations of the symbols, but what they meant, he could not guess.

Tim Oats was vastly intrigued. "That there's valuable," he declared. "I began life workin' with metals, worked for a jeweler, I did, an' whoever put that thing together was a craftsman! He really knew what he was doin'!"

"It isn't Latin," White said irritably. "It isn't any language I know."

"It's old," Oats said, "but there's not a speck of rust. I heard tell of iron like that made long ago in India."

"A children's toy," Brunn had written in his notes, "of only family interest."

James White, a devious man himself, did not accept that conclusion. In the weeks since it had come into his possession, he had moved, twisted, and turned it—but to no avail. If it had a secret, it was beyond him.

Since three thousand dollars represented four to five years of income for James White, he had no intention of giving it up to any ignorant hillbilly girl. He stared at the papers on his desk and swore bitterly. Three thousand dollars to that impudent slip of a girl! It was preposterous!

Yet, suppose he had to pay it to her? What then? It was a long way back to Tennessee, most of it by stage. White rubbed his jaw thoughtfully, then brushed his mustache with a forefinger.

Maybe . . . just maybe. . . .


Finian Chantry entered the library of the club and looked about. He nodded here and there to the regulars, men with whom he frequently had dealings, business or political, most of whom he had known for years, and in some cases their fathers before them. When his wife had been alive, they dined out often, but of late he had become more and more of a recluse, preferring his books to most of the conversation about matters whose conclusions were obvious.

The club was different. It was one place that held no memories of his wife. It was a gathering place for men, and men only. As he grew older he liked less and less to be involved in disagreements of any kind, and here, in the quiet precincts of the club, over brandy and cigars, he had settled some of his most difficult cases.

It was easier, sometimes, to meet with people on neutral ground, to discuss probable outcomes and resolve problems without going to court. Chantry was, as they all knew, a thorough student of the law, who prepared his cases with infinite skill. His memory was fantastic and he seemed to forget nothing, recalling with ease rulings made fifty years before. He seemed to have read everything and forgotten nothing. Most other attorneys preferred to settle his cases out of court rather than go to trial and almost certain defeat.

Pendleton was a cheerful man with a bald head and muttonchop whiskers. He glanced up as Chantry approached.

"Finian! Come and sit down! We don't see much of you these days!"

"Busy, George, busy! Reading a lot, too. This fellow Dickens, you know? The Englishman?"

"Indeed, I do know! My wife and daughter can scarcely wait for the ship to get in with the next installment. Pity we don't have such writers here!"

Chantry seated himself. "George, do you know anything about a lawyer named White? James White?"

"I know him." He twisted in his seat and spoke to the black waiter who was approaching. "Archie? Get Mr. Chantry something, will you? And bring us some cigars."

"Calvados, sir?"

"Please."

"White's a scoundrel. Be disbarred one of these days. Mixes in all sorts of shady dealings. Nothing we can do about it, but we're watching the man."

When the calvados arrived, Finian took but a sip before putting down his glass. He drank rarely, but the apple brandy from Normandy seemed about right. He accepted a cigar, bit off the end, and accepted a light from Archie.

"He is handling an estate in which a client of mine is interested."

"Your client should be careful. The man's a shyster. If not an actual criminal." Pendleton drew on his cigar. "Some of Adam Brunn's business, I suspect. When Adam died, his widow put the business in White's hands—why, I can't imagine.

"Adam was a nice old gentleman, but when he died, his widow asked White to handle his affairs. I heard her housekeeper recommended White."

Pendleton glanced at Chantry. "A client of yours, you say? I didn't know you handled cases of that sort."

"The client is a young lady who walked in out of nowhere."

"With White involved? I'd be careful, Finian. You are a wealthy man, you know."

"Nothing like that. She recognized my nameplate and came for advice, as she did not trust White. She had recognized the name, and as soon as she mentioned hers, it took me back. I knew her grandfather, George, knew him in the war, and had it not been for him, I'd not be here at all."

"The war?"

"The Revolution. He was from Tennessee. The greatest woodsman I ever met or expect to meet. We met by accident, but he had known my older brother, had dealings with him. In fact, there's been a shadowy connection between our families for many years. I expect it happens more often than we realize, but our families have rubbed elbows a dozen times."

"What is the nature of her problem?"

"She did not trust the man. Instinct, I guess, although one of the boarders at Mrs. Sulky's warned her."

Chantry tasted the calvados again. "The Sacketts are

an odd lot, George. No sooner did they get ashore in this country than they headed for the hills. Like homing pigeons. Once there, they took to the wilderness as if born to it.

"This young lady comes from a place called Tuckalucky Cove. Never been out of the hills except for one short trip to visit relatives in Charleston. But she's no fool. Canny little thing, and afraid of nothing."

"A little fear might do her good."

Chantry chuckled. "Might, but I doubt it. If she is like the other Sacketts I've known, it is the others who should have a little fear."

"White's a bad actor. Remember Felix Horst? Involved in some killings down along the river a few years ago? Escaped from prison while awaiting trial? White was suspected of arranging his escape."

"Ah? Yes, I do recall something of the kind. Well, I am glad she came to me. I doubt if he will attempt anything if she arrives at his office with me."

"You are going with her?"

"She's a child, George. Only sixteen. Of course I shall go." He brushed the ash from his cigar. "By the way, George, that clerk of yours who is reading law? I believe his name is Gibbons?"

"Johnny Gibbons?" Pendleton was surprised. "What about him?"

"Did he not work for Adam Brunn before he came to you? I would like to talk to him."

"Well, I suppose it could be arranged. Come to think of it, he did work for Brunn." He glanced up. "Imagine you remembering that."

"Tonight, George? I would like to see him tonight."

Pendleton glanced at his watch. "Finian, you are a most difficult man. I should have known you had something on your mind."

Reluctantly Pendleton got to his feet. "I don't know. I could send a messenger—"

"We shall go ourselves. Or rather, I shall. I do not wish to interrupt your dinner."

"But—"

"Don't worry about it. I shall go myself, if you will just tell me where to find him."

"Sir, you cannot consider such a thing! Gibbons fancies himself as a writer. Oh, he's reading law, all right, and a very astute young man he is, but he is also planning a book on Philadelphia's history as a seaport. He will not be in his room tonight, but in some dive on the waterfront."

"Very well, then that is where I shall go. I must see him. He will certainly know something of the Sackett case, and I must have the information before calling upon White."

"Sir?" Chantry turned at Archie's voice. "I could go with you, sir. I shall be finished here in a few minutes, and I know the waterfront well. I went to sea at one time."

"Thank you, Archie, I shall appreciate the company."

The big black man hesitated. "You know, sir, it is very rough down there?"

"Archie, I am an old man now, but I, too, spent time at sea."

"Very well, sir."

"Do you know Johnny Gibbons?"

"I do sir. There are only a few places he might be, where seamen gather and he can pick up the stories."

Finian Chantry waited at the door for his carriage and for Archie to join him. He felt oddly exhilarated. How many years since he had walked the waterfront? Too many years, far too many.

"You are eighty-six years old, Finian," he said to himself, "of no age to go to the sort of places you will be going tonight. I wonder just how much is left of that young man who commanded his own vessel? Have the years carried it all down the drain? Or is there something left?"

He wore the long trousers that had come in shortly after the beginning of the century, and a top hat. He carried a cane . . . was never without it.

"Sir?" Archie spoke quietly. "We must be careful. There are men down there who would murder you for a shilling, a guilder, or a dollar."

"I have met them before, Archie, when I was younger. I am an old man now, but I wonder how old."

# 4

They found Johnny Gibbons seated over a mug of ale in the Dutchman's, on Dock Street. The room was crowded with a sweating, smoking, drinking mélange of seafaring men from Copenhagen to Cape Town and all the ports between. They were men from ships which came in with the tide and would be off again in a day or a week. They came ashore for the women, the whiskey, rum, or gin, and some even made it back to their own vessels. Others were shanghaied by crimps and awakened in a dirty bunk aboard a ship strange to them, their belongings lost to them, their future in doubt.

Finian Chantry pushed the door open with his cane and stepped into the room, recognizing Gibbons at once. That young man glanced up, his eyes riveted, and his mouth dropped open in astonishment. Archie led the way through the crowded room.

Finian glanced around, enjoying himself, then seated himself opposite Johnny Gibbons.

Johnny was embarrassed and worried. "Sir? With all

due respect, you shouldn't have come to this place! It is dangerous, sir. There are a lot of honest seamen here, but almost as many crimps and thieves."

"Johnny, I spent my youth in such places. In and out of them, at least. I commanded my own ship with crews who were more than half of them pirates."

"I know, sir, but—"

"Johnny, you worked for Adam Brunn? Do you remember the O'Hara case?"

"Of course, sir. It was the last case on which I was employed. One of the O'Haras, the last of that line, I believe, was a friend of Mr. Brunn. It seems the first of their family had been beholden to Barnabas Sackett, and very close to Barnabas's son, Kin. Several times over the years there was contact between the families, but the last O'Hara willed what was left to the last descendant of Kin Sackett."

"The sum?"

"Something over three thousand dollars. Nowadays that's quite a sum, but the money was the least of it. There was an iron cube, some sort of a Chinese puzzle. He opened it and showed us what was inside. It was a sapphire, a big one, couldn't have weighed less than twenty carats. He showed it to Mr. Brunn and me and then returned it to the box, made a few deft twists concealed by his palms, and handed it over to Brunn.

"When Adam Brunn died, his widow turned his business over to White. I protested, but Mrs. Brunn listened to this woman who worked for her who was always telling her what a wonderful man White was.

"I had given my notice before the old man died, as I wanted to set up for myself, and she would not listen to me. She resented the fact that I was going on my own, although Mr. Brunn did not. You see, I did not want to practice the kind of law he did. He had a very quiet, secure sort of business, but I wanted to be where things were happening. And I wished to write."

"Thank you. I believe you have told me what I need to know. I think we should go now."

"May I come with you? I've noticed, sir, some very rough characters have been watching you. You dress too well to be walking around down here."

"Come, if you will. It is only a few blocks to where my carriage waits, and I have Archie with me."

As they left the Dutchman's, Finian saw a side door back of the bar open and close, and he smiled a little to himself. You are an old fool, Finian, he told himself, to be thinking such thoughts at your age!

When they reached the corner a block from the Dutchman's, they saw three men under the gaslight. The three glanced their way, then turned and walked along ahead of them.

"Did you see them, Archie?"

"I did, sir. There may be trouble."

"It has been a long time since I have had that kind of trouble, Archie. I have often wondered how I would react."

"Sir?" Gibbons said. "One of those men up ahead is Bully Benson—he's a thug and a murderer. If I am not mistaken, there will be others behind us."

"Of course, Johnny. Be careful, now. I grew up on this sort of thing. There was that night in Bombay—"

"There they are, sir. They are waiting for us."

"Johnny, you and Archie take care of those behind us. Leave the three in front to me. I shall take it as a favor."

"Sir, you are eighty-six years old! Please, sir—"

"Years of experience, Johnny. I think we shall surprise them."

"He fences every day at the club," Archie said. "There's nobody there can handle him. Not even those young naval officers."

They rounded the corner and three rough-looking characters were spread across the walk before them.

Finian smiled. "Good evening, gentlemen! Is there something we can do for you?"

"You can hand over d' gelt, d' coin! An' quick!"

Finian Chantry held his cane in two hands and smiled.
"Ah? You hear him, Johnny? The man's threatening
me!" His eyes went from one to the other. "And if I
don't choose to?"

"We'll bust your damn skull!"

"You're Benson, I take it? Well, Benson, I'll give you
a chance. Turn about now and run. Get away from here
while you can, and we'll make believe this never
happened."

"Blimey! Would y' listen to that? The old gent's
balmy! He's off his bloody course, he is!"

"You're a pack of bilge-swilling swine!" Chantry said.
"I've money enough in my pockets to keep you drunk
for a month of Sundays, but if you come for it, you'll be
wearing your guts for neckties!"

One of the men started to back off. "Listen t' him,
Bully! This one's no gent! Let's get out of here!"

"If I had the lot of you aboard a ship of mine," Finian
said cheerfully, "I'd have you kissing the gunner's
daughter! You'd be bent over a starb'rd gun getting fifty
good ones on the backside from a Penang lawyer!"

"Bully? Let's get out of here! This one's walked a
deck of his own!"

"Don't be a damn fool! S'pose he has? I want that
. . . All *right! Take him!*"

The shout was accompanied by a lunge. The second
man leaped, swinging a cudgel. Bully Benson held a
knife.

Finian Chantry's brain was icy. He took a half-step
back and the cane seemed to spring apart in his hands.
A blade leaped from the cane like a whip of dancing
light. Benson caught the flash of the blade and tried to
pull up, his eyes bulging with sheer horror. The next
moment, where his mouth had been there was an ugly
gash as the blade cut ear to ear. The second man swung

his cudgel, but the sweeping blade had never stopped moving, slicing his cheek and nicking his nose.

He screamed and dropped his club, both hands going to his face. Bully Benson was already in a staggering run, choking on his own blood. The third and wiser man had never closed, and he was maintaining a fair lead as he ran.

Turning quickly, Finian saw Johnny Gibbons had a man against the wall and was slugging him with both fists. Archie had put one man down, and the third was running away.

Finian Chantry's heart was pounding as he watched them go; then, taking a handkerchief from his pocket, he wiped clean the sword blade and returned it to the cane. "A pack of scoundrels," he commented as Johnny Gibbons came up beside him. "This will give them something to consider before they try it again."

When they reached the carriage, Chantry got in and Johnny followed. "Archie?" he invited.

"Thank you, sir, your coachman is a friend, I shall ride out with him."

"Back there," Gibbons commented, "you spoke of giving that chap fifty good ones with a 'Penang lawyer.' I had never heard the phrase."

"A Penang lawyer is a strip of rattan. It was used to influence discipline aboard craft in the Indian Ocean."

"You were a ship's officer?"

"Briefly. Like my brother, I was a merchant venturer, investing in cargoes and often going along to handle the trading myself. I had read for the law, as had he, so I finally settled for that. It was a fortunate choice."

"In the O'Hara affair, if I can be of any assistance, you have only to ask."

"No, it is a small matter. What you have told me is sufficient."

Alone in his bedroom, Finian Chantry looked down upon his hands. "Useful," he muttered, "useful still. And there was no fear, that is important."

He felt no sympathy for Bully Benson. They had chosen the time, the place, and their weapons. What they got was less than what they deserved.

At supper I was seated in the same place, and discovered that in boardinghouses as at home, most people wanted to sit in the same seats. The bald-headed man who sat across from me was named Prescott. He nodded and smiled when I came in. "How are you enjoying Philadelphia?" he asked.

"There's so much to see! After I saw Mr. White and Mr. Chantry—"

The fat man farther down the table looked up from his food long enough to give me a sharp, somewhat impatient glance. He clutched his knife and fork as if prepared for battle. "Chantry, did you say? You *saw* Finian Chantry?"

"I did. He was very nice."

"Young lady"—he spoke with authority—"you must be mistaken. Nobody, but *no*body just walks in and sees Finian Chantry."

"I saw him. I shall see him again in the morning. He is coming with me to see Mr. White."

Very patiently the man said, "Miss Sackett, I know very important men who have tried for *weeks* to see Mr. Chantry. He is a busy man and accepts no new clients. You must have met somebody else who you assumed was Finian Chantry."

He resumed eating and for a moment I thought of replying, then thought it was no use. And what did it matter, anyway?

Amy Sulky came in and seated herself. "Echo, there's a man in the sitting room who wishes to speak to you. His name is White. He said you would know him, but I told him we were at supper and he could not see you until it was over."

Mr. Prescott said, "Miss Sackett? If I can be of service? A witness or something?"

"Thank you. I cannot imagine why Mr. White is here. We were to meet in the morning, when Mr. Chantry can be there."

The man down the table gave me an exasperated glance, but his mouth was full as usual and he said nothing. I am sure he wished to. He was called Mr. Butts, and judging by the size of his stomach, he was a very important man. He mopped the gravy from his plate with a piece of bread and looked enviously across the table at the skinny young man's plate whose meal was only half-eaten.

Amy Sulky arose. "If I can help in any way . . . ?" she paused, lifting her eyebrows in question.

"No, ma'am. I have met him before. It will be all right."

White got quickly to his feet when I came into the room. "Ah! Miss Sackett! How good of you to see me! Knowing how anxious you were to return to your mountains, I thought I had best do as much as possible to expedite your trip.

"I have the money here, and you've only to sign a release and you can be on your way. A receipt, that is."

Taking from his pocket a small sack, he began counting out gold pieces on the table. For a moment I could only stare. Never before in my life had I seen even one gold piece, and here they were in shining stacks, and all mine. It was unbelievable.

He placed a sheet of paper on the table before me.

All I could think of was the gold and what it would do for all of us, and I wished that Pa had lived until now.

Mr. White dipped a pen in the inkwell and handed it to me. "Just sign right there"—he put a pudgy finger on the line—"just sign right there and it is all yours."

He pushed a stack of the gold toward me, and I reached for the pen.

# 5

First I sat down and looked at that paper. Five hundred dollars in gold was a sight of money, and it would do a lot for my folks, but I did not like that bit about "paid in full." How did I know that was all there was? And Mr. Prescott, him with the bald head and the beard, he had said, "Don't sign anything."

"Mr. White," I said, "I can't do it. I talked to Finian Chantry and he is coming to your office with me tomorrow morning. There's no reason why I can't wait until then."

His mean little eyes tightened a bit around the edges. "Miss Sackett"—he held his voice patient—"I do not have time to waste. I have brought you the money, five hundred dollars in gold. Sign that paper and it is yours.

"I won't," he added, "even deduct the cost of advertising or my expenses. You can have it all."

Whenever a man like James White gets generous, a body had better hold on to his pocketbook. "No, I've

35

asked Mr. Chantry to handle it for me. It wouldn't be polite if I went ahead without him."

"Finian Chantry," White said impatiently, "is too busy to bother with any mountain girl. You are just using his name. Now, you just sign that paper. I have another appointment and I simply can't wait."

"Tomorrow morning. Finian Chantry will be with me. We can get it all straightened out in a few minutes."

He stared at me; then he got up. "You've had your chance," he said. "You may never see that gold again. I have no idea what your Finian Chantry hopes to do—"

A voice spoke from behind me. It was the tall young man from down the table. "Mister, if I were you, I would leave that gold with the young lady. Anybody who carries that much in the streets at night is crazy."

James White ignored him. He pushed the paper at me again, and then the pen. "If you want that money," he said, "you had better sign."

"I am sorry, sir." I got to my feet. "Not until tomorrow morning."

He got up too, and he was almighty angry, I could see that. His face was flushed a mean red and he glared at me. "You are a very stubborn, foolish young lady, and you may lose it all."

The young man had moved up beside me, and Mr. Prescott had come into the room. He said, "If the money is due her," he said, "you will have it or the courts will take steps to recover it."

He glared at us, then put the money back in the black bag he was carrying and without another word went out and slammed the door.

"Thank you," I said.

"So that is James White?" Mr. Prescott said. "I have heard of him. If you wish, I could arrange the time to accompany you?"

"No, thanks. Mr. Chantry will be there."

We talked a few minutes and they left, going to their

rooms. For a few minutes I just stood there staring
down at where all that gold had been.

Had I been a fool? Just think! Tomorrow morning I
could have been on a stage starting for home again.
Now how long would it be? And would I get any money
at all? What the law said, I had no idea, and maybe
there were ways he could keep it, and I would have to
return with empty pockets.

That night, lying in bed, I worried myself to sleep.
Mr. Chantry was an old man and he looked frail for all
that he was tall and moved well. Suppose there was
violence? Where I came from in the mountains, there
was often bloodshed over such things, and I did not
know how it would be in Philadelphia. When I got up
in the morning, I would check my pistol.

Mr. White was stocky, and although a mite thick in
the middle, he looked strong. And there was that man
who followed me. I should have told Mr. Chantry about
him.


When morning came, and when I had my breakfast, I
sat waiting in the sitting room. I was wearing a poke
bonnet and a long full skirt trimmed with bows of
ribbon and a shawl around my shoulders. My knitting
bag was on my lap and my pick was inside my skirt in
its scabbard and ready to hand. A girl can't be too
careful.

Mr. Butts came in, picking his teeth with an ivory
toothpick. He glanced at me irritably. "I am surprised,"
he said. "You should have taken the money he brought."

"Five hundred dollars? It's more than I earn in a
year! Preposterous!"

"I think she did the right thing, Mr. Butts," Mrs.
Sulky said. "Why would he come over here at night to
get her to sign those papers? They had an appointment
for today."

"She will wind up with nothing, nothing at all!"

There was a tap at the door, and when Amy Sulky opened it, Finian Chantry was there, a tall, elegant old man in a gray frock coat and trousers of a lighter gray.

"Mrs. Sulky? Mr. Chantry."

"How do you do?"

"Mr. Chantry?" Mr. Butts thrust himself forward. "I am Ephraim Butts, and I have been hoping to have a chance to speak to you—"

"Another time, Mr. Butts. Miss Sackett and I have business to discuss." He stepped back to allow me to precede him. "Miss Sackett?"

When we were seated in his carriage, I said, "I don't like that man."

"Do not let yourself be bothered by the inconsequential. One has only so much time in this world, so devote it to the work and the people most important to you, to those you love and things that matter. One can waste half a lifetime with people one doesn't really like, or doing things when one would be better off somewhere else."

As we rode along over the brick-paved streets, I told him about James White coming to the boardinghouse with the five hundred dollars.

"You did the right thing, Echo," he said. "There is much more involved."

He stepped down from the carriage at Mr. White's office and shifted his cane to the other hand to help me down. "That's a beautiful cane," I said. "My father had one like it."

"Yes, I shouldn't wonder. Inherited from your grandfather, perhaps?"

"Yes, I believe it was, although Pa never had much use for it. He was always a strong walker."

"Of course." He held the cane up. "It is just a little something I like to have with me. It has become a habit, I am afraid."

The tall, dirty-looking young man stood up quickly when he saw Mr. Chantry. "Yes, sir!"

"Mr. White, if you please. Miss Sackett and Finian Chantry to see him."

"Yes, sir. Right away, sir."

White sat hunched behind his desk when we entered. He stood up grudgingly. "Mr. Chantry? What can I do for you, sir?"

"You can pay Miss Sackett three thousand, three hundred and twenty-five dollars. This is, I believe, the sum due her from the estate of Barnabas O'Hara, deceased."

"Now, see here! I—"

"Mr. White, I am not a very patient man. As I grow older, I find time very important. I also have had occasion to discuss some of your activities with various members of the bar. Miss Sackett has apprised me of your attempt to get her to sign away most of her inheritance, and I am in no mood for dillydallying. The money, sir!"

Reluctantly White got up and went to his safe. For a moment he hesitated; then he turned the handle and opened the door.

When he had counted the money, he pushed it across the desk. "There!" he said. "Now, here's the receipt."

"One thing more." Finian Chantry's voice was cold. "The iron puzzle cube."

White gripped the edge of his desk. He stared at Chantry, trying to frighten him. "That cube? It's nothing but a child's toy."

"My client likes toys, and she is very good at puzzles, Mr. White. The cube, please."

White returned to the safe and brought the cube to the desk. "It isn't anything." He waved a careless hand. "Just a sort of puzzle for youngsters."

"Thank you, Mr. White." Chantry turned to me. "Now, Miss Sackett? Will you sign his paper?"


When we were seated in the carriage, Finian Chantry suggested, "Now that your business is over, would you consent to have dinner with me? You have no idea what it would do for me to be seen with such a young and beautiful lady."

Well! An elegant supper with Finian Chantry! When I was back in my room, I got out the dress I had made for just such an evening. It was not a dress made for this trip, but one I had made after dreaming of all those fancy places Regal had talked about.

*Godey's* had a lot of pictures of dresses, although none of them had much of an explanation, and Regal was no help at all.

Amy Sulky helped, and then—and I was fairly amazed— the tall woman who I'd said looked like she was weaned on a sour pickle, she came to help.

She was much better at pressing than I was, and she ironed out my dress. Then she said, "Where are your gloves?"

"Gloves?" I stared, in a sudden panic.

"You must have gloves. No lady of fashion appears in public without them!"

In the end, she loaned me a beautiful shawl. "From India," she said, with no explanation at all. And she loaned me some lace mittens which were all the fashion. The shawl was rich cashmere, almost too beautiful to touch.

The dress was a full triple skirt, blue as the sky. I'd only two petticoats, so the sour-pickle lady, whose name turned out to be Alicia, loaned me another. Oddly enough, although she was tall, the petticoat was perfect for me.

When I spoke of it, she said, with never a flicker of expression, "It belonged to my daughter."

"Oh! I hope she won't mind."

"My daughter is dead." She spoke flatly and turned away. I did not know what to say, so I said nothing at all.

When I was all ready and waiting for Mr. Chantry, both Amy and Alicia stood waiting with me. "You are

very beautiful," Alicia said. "You should stay in Philadelphia."

"I love the mountains, and besides, while Regal is
laid up, who would hunt for them?"

"You mean you *hunt*? You? You actually kill things?"

"Yes, ma'am. Whatever meat we have is wild meat,
shot by me when the boys are away. We have hogs,
razorbacks they call them, but they run wild in the
forest and we only gather them up to sell them in town.
There's no more fun ever than being on a hog or turkey
drive, going miles across the hills to the towns.

"That is, it's a sight of fun while the weather's nice,
but if it comes on to rain, it can be awful. We have to
find a place to pen them for the night. Mostly folks
along the way are helpful, but if a body's caught in the
forest, it can be right mean."

There I was standing in my triple skirt with lace
mittens and all, that auburn hair which everybody says
is beautiful falling over my shoulders, and talking of
driving wild hogs and hunting game.

"If I were you," Amy advised, "I'd say nothing of
driving hogs to the people you may meet tonight. They
wouldn't understand."

"Yes, ma'am, but ever'body in the mountains does
what's necessary."

The United States Hotel served up a supper the like
of which I'd never seen, and we had Mumm's cham-
pagne to drink, which cost two dollars and a half a
bottle!

"Do you have wine in the mountains?" Mr. Chantry
asked.

"Some do," I admitted, "but mostly folks drink cider
or whiskey of their own make. At least, the menfolks
do.

"There's wild grapes in the mountains, and there
have been some planted here and there. Some folks
have made wine, but not such as this."

*Two dollars and a half a bottle!* That was outrageous.

In the mountains a body could buy a barrel of whiskey for that price.

"I never paid much mind to it, Mr. Chantry," I said. "Womenfolks in the mountains in our time don't touch whiskey. At least, not in public. There are some who like a little nip on the sly, but not me. None of our family were drinkers, although I've heard tell that wild Clinch Mountain bunch would tap the jug once in a while."

"You must be careful," Mr. Chantry warned. "You'll be carrying quite a lot of money, and I shall be surprised if there isn't an attempt to rob you."

"I came a long way to get this money, and I don't intend to let no thief take it from me. I've got a pistol, and I have my pick."

"Oh, yes. The pick." Finian Chantry had a nice smile. "But be careful. That's a lot of money to most people."

We had mock turtle soup, boiled bluefish with oyster sauce, tomatoes, and eggplant.

Mr. Chantry asked me about the mountains, so I told him about our cabin in the laurel with pines along the ridge above, the clear cold spring that gave us water, and the hole near the spring where we kept our butter and milk. I told him about hunting game and of the Clinch Mountain boys who were raised on bear meat and poke greens.

"There was a time we could have become rich folk. The land was for the taking, but we taken more to hunting along the ridges than settling in the rich bottomlands. Of a sudden the rich land was gone and all that was left was ridges and high country."

Across the room a man had been seated facing us. He was a tall man with high cheekbones, a beak of a nose, and thin, tight lips. When I looked over, he was staring at us, and he turned his eyes away, but I had seen the look. He was a hunter.

"Mr. Chantry, there's a man across the room, just

beyond the gray-haired man with the two ladies. I figure him for trouble."

After a moment, Finian Chantry looked over and said, "You are a very perceptive young lady. That is Felix Horst. James White defended him once . . . for murder."

# 6

We took our time over supper. There was music playing somewhere out of sight—mighty pleasant it was, too. Most folks dined at home, but there were always a few who wished to go out to eat. The waiters went about their business so quietly a body scarcely realized they were about. Meanwhile, I kept an eye on Felix Horst.

It was unlikely his being here was an accident. He had been sent to prison for murder but James White had got the case reopened and contrived to free him. Maybe it was happenstance that he was having supper at the same time and place as me just after I had come into money, but I didn't believe it.

Murder didn't scare me the way it did most folks. Cuttings and shootings were common back in the hills, and we even had a feud of our own, with some killings over the years.

From time to time folks stopped by our table, and Mr. Chantry introduced me as the granddaughter of an old friend. A good many of them were younger men, mighty fetching in their ways.

Three of them sat at a table not far off, but only two paid their respects, as the saying was. The other young man sat with his back to us, very broad in the shoulders, and he looked to be tall, although I did not see him on his feet.

"My nephew, Dorian," Finian Chantry explained. "He will not come to our table because we have recently had words and he is a very independent young man."

Mr. Chantry smiled suddenly, a mischievous glint in his eyes. "We are much alike, so we do have words occasionally. Lately he has been devoting more time to dancing, riding to hounds, fencing and such things, and not studying law."

"He is a good shot?"

"Excellent, I believe, and a fine horseman, too. He is a great favorite with the ladies and a bit too sure of himself. Nonetheless, he's a fine lad if a little too formal, too stiff."

Mr. Chantry glanced at me. "You mentioned your rifle? Do you shoot?"

"Yes, sir. Pa started me shooting when I was seven. Those brothers of mine had been riding roughshod over me because I was a girl.

"Pa, he said, 'Look, bein' a girl is a mighty fine thing. Don't let those roughneck brothers of yours get the better of you.'

" 'How can I help it? They are older than me and stronger than me.'

" 'Be better than they are. Learn to shoot better.'

" 'How can I? Nobody can shoot better than a Sackett!'

"He laughed at me and said, 'But you're a Sackett too! Just learn to shoot better. Here, I'll teach you!' And he did."

"And did you beat them?"

"Yes, sir. Most of the time. Only Regal . . . he's my uncle, although more like a brother. Regal would not shoot against me. I think he did not want to beat me, seeing I just outshot my brothers."

"Maybe that is what Dorian needs, to be outshot by a girl."

"Oh, no! I'd never do that! Regal, he warned me to never let a man know how good I could shoot."

"Good advice, but don't let it stop you. Dorian's a fine lad. What he needs is seasoning. He needs to be taken down a bit, to travel some rough country."

Later, when I glanced over to catch a glimpse of him, he had gone. I felt kind of let down.

We talked on for a bit and then Mr. Chantry said, "You surprise me sometimes. You can speak very good English, but sometimes you talk like a mountain girl with no education."

"Yes, sir, but that's the way with most folks, if you think on it. They talk one way to one person, and another way to others.

"Ma insisted I learn to talk proper, and at school it was insisted on, but when around the hills, a body gets to talkin' as they do. But it seems to me we all have several ways of talkin' or writin'. Take you, for example, you bein' a lawyer. You have a set of law words you'd use in court but not over supper like this. And when a body writes a letter, he often uses words he wouldn't use in conversation.

"Down to the store, the men set about talking of politics, planting, the wars, Injuns and suchlike, and most of them can argue the Bible up one side an' down the other. Because a man doesn't speak good English doesn't mean he doesn't have ideas.

"Our atheist, he's a book-learned man. Nothing folks like better than to get him and the preacher talking history and religion. They'll argue sundown to sunup, and folks settin' about listenin'. There's old Mr. Fothergill, he was in the army as a boy and went upon the sea a time or two. He can't read nor write but he's bright, an' he can argue down both of them when he wants.

"Some folks think that being smart in the books is the only kind of smart, but that just isn't so. Men learn a lot by doin', and they learn by listenin' to what others say, but when a man is workin' on a farm or walkin' in the woods or ridin' across country, he can do a lot of thinking. Many a man who reads a lot just repeats what he's read, and not what he thinks.

"It seems to me," I added, "that a body may have a dozen sets of words he uses on occasion. Anyway, lots of men who work at hand labor have read a good bit and can talk of things far from their work."

Given a chance, I changed the subject, because this was about as good a chance as I would get to learn more about grandfather.

"Yes," Mr. Chantry replied when asked, "you are right in what you say. Daubeny Sackett was such a man. He was the finest woodsman I ever knew, and a fantastic shot with a rifle, but when the occasion demanded, he could discuss government or philosophy with the best. He had read few books, I believe, but had read them several times. But that was the way of it in those days.

"He was at the Battle of King's Mountain and at Cowpens also. I last saw him at the surrender of Cornwallis at Yorktown.

"He knew them all, you know. Washington, Jefferson, Patrick Henry, George Mason. . . . He was quite a man, your grandfather."

He ordered more coffee and I glanced over at the table where the three young men had been. Other folks sat there now.

"Echo? What are your plans? You could stay here, you know. There are several very fine schools for young ladies, and from the attention you are attracting from the young men, I cannot imagine you would be lonely."

"No, sir. I shall head for the hills again when morning comes. The folks back home will wonder how I am faring."

"You could stay, you know. I have a very large, very empty house, and Mary Brennan—she's my house-keeper—would love to have you to fuss over. I am afraid I demand too little of her time."

"Thank you, sir. I'm a-longing for the smell of the pines, and I want to see the clouds gatherin' over Clingman's Dome.

"You should come a-callin' sometime when the leaves are falling and it gets on to storytellin' time. Most of our young-uns learn their history from stories told by the fireside. It isn't the history you folks know, but it's the story of people we know or our grandfolks knew.

"Wars aren't far-off things to us. Pa fit in the War of 1812. He was with the Kentucky riflemen who stood behind the bales of cotton at New Orleans. When fightin' men were needed, there was always a Sackett to be found."

Mr. Chantry, I thought, was a lonely man, and when we lingered at table it was because he wished to pro-long the time. I knew how he felt, because many a time when we'd set by the fire telling stories or singin' the old ballads like "Greensleeves" or "Barbry Allen," I wished it would never end.

"I miss my wife, Echo," he said suddenly. "You are so like her, so very feminine." He glanced at me, a glint of amusement in his eyes. "Somehow, I cannot imagine you with a rifle."

"I grew up with one, used a rifle as soon as a needle. I used to walk the woods to school, or canoe on the rivers, and when a girl's much alone, she becomes independent. I've camped out in the woods when caught by storms. It never worried me much."

"You leave in the morning?"

"Yes, sir. I have already booked passage on the stage."

"You must be careful. You will be carrying what is a

great deal of money to some people, and that little iron box could buy you a farm in the flatlands, and a big farm at that.

"Felix Horst is still here, and I do not believe it is an accident. He owes White a favor and he is a dangerous man. I wish you would change your mind and stay with me."

"If Horst comes after me for the money," I said, "I think it will be for himself. He looks like a meaner man than Mr. White. He'd rob a man quick enough, I think, and kill him, too. Once I get in the woods, I won't be worried about such as him."

Mr. Chantry smiled, shaking his head. "You Sacketts! You always amaze me!"

"We live in wild country, sir. I know folks who think all wild things are sweet and cuddly, but they've never come into a henhouse after a weasel has been there. He can drink the blood of only one or two, but often as not he'll kill every one of them. Wolves will do it in a pen of lambs, too. There are savage beasts in the world, Mr. Chantry, and men who are just as savage. We've come upon them now and again."

Well, I switched the subject to pleasanter things and got him to telling me of his courtship and how he proposed and all. When he stopped the carriage at Mrs. Sulky's, it was mighty late. As the carriage moved away, something stirred in the shadows across the street.

The trouble was, when I snuggled down in bed, I wasn't thinking of the stage that would take me west to Pittsburgh, but of the back of that young man's head and those broad shoulders. The trouble was, I'd probably never see him again, or get to know him.

Amy Sulky was in the kitchen when I came down the stairs before daybreak. She was there working with the black woman who did most of the cooking. She was a free woman wedded to a man who was coachman for a wealthy family. They went to the door with me and Amy fretted some. "I don't like it! You going home alone, all that way! And you carrying money!"

"The less said of it, the better," I cautioned. "But don't you worry none. I've been about the mountains more than a bit."

We said our good-byes and I taken up my carpetbag, a good bit heavier now, but nothing I couldn't handle. Back in the hills I'd rustled stumps and logs for the fire more than once, and was accustomed to carryin' weight.

First off, I taken a good look about, but saw nobody watching me.

At the coach house there was a goodly crowd, but it was not until I was seated that I saw that man with the hard gray hat and the houndstooth coat a-settin' in the corner of the mail coach across from me, but in the farthest corner. There were twelve passengers, and the rest seemed what a body would expect. Five were women, aside from me, but only one who was youngish. She was a pert, pretty girl with big eyes and a friendly smile.

Seated close beside me was a little old lady with gray hair and quick blue eyes.

We started at a brisk pace, but the road was rough and we bounced around a good deal, which would have been worse but for the bulky sacks of mail crowded in with us. That little old lady was crowded right up to me, and once, glancing down, I noticed that her carpetbag, a new one, was just like mine.

Several times I sneaked a look at the man in the gray hat and houndstooth coat, but he was looking out the window and paying me no mind. It could be he was on business of his own and I was just too suspicious. Nevertheless, I decided to stay suspicious.

We passed several wagons with families bound to the westward, the men walking, the women and children inside. Mostly they were Conestoga wagons, big, strongly built, and built to float if need be. Mostly these folks, according to one of the men on the coach, were heading for Illinois or Missouri. A man named Birkbeck had been settling folks on land he had in Illinois.

We stopped to let off a couple of people in Lancaster, and pick up one more. Regal was forever talking about the fine rifles made at this place by the Pennsylvania Dutch. At least, that's what he called them.

My thoughts kept straying back to that young man in the dining room that night. Dorian Chantry. It was a nice name. I minded what Regal said, "Don't be in no hurry. You'll meet a hundred men, maybe one or two of them worthwhile and of the right age."

"What's the right age?" I had asked him.

"You'll know when you see him," he said, grinning at me.

It was late, so I didn't see much of Lancaster, but we stopped for more than an hour in Elizabeth Town and I carried my bag with me to the place where we could get coffee, bread, and some slices of beef. The little old lady had come from the stage too, and she sat near me, smiling very pleasantly but keeping to herself and showing no mood for talk.

We passed through several towns, none of them far apart, and it was not until Chambersburg that we stopped for the night. By that time we were dead beat. I was so tired of being jounced around that I scarcely could move. I saw the man in the houndstooth coat help that little old lady down from the carriage, taking her bag from her in kindly fashion. Maybe I was mistaken about him.

Picking up my bag, I started for the door to step down, but the bag felt funny. I looked down, and in the dim light it looked all right. Somebody helped me down and I picked up the bag again.

It was too light. Opening it, I taken one look. It wasn't my bag!

Horrified, I looked up just in time to see the man in the houndstooth coat and that little old lady vanishing around a corner! He was carrying my bag.

# 7

Finian Chantry looked up from his desk as the door opened. Slowly he jostled the papers together until the ends squared, then placed them to one side.

Dorian Chantry was a tall, athletic young man, not unlike he himself at that age, although, Finian admitted, Dorian was a bit broader in the shoulders and somewhat more muscular than he himself had been.

"I have a mission for you."

"A mission? Or do you mean a job?" Dorian revealed even white teeth in a flashing smile.

"A mission. Did you happen to see the young lady who was with me last night at supper?"

"Everybody else was paying attention. It seemed to me she could do without mine."

"Then you would not recognize her if you saw her?"

"I would not."

"She left town this morning carrying something over three thousand dollars and a gem in a small iron box just about three inches by two. I am worried about her."

Dorian Chantry drew back a chair and sat down. "Uncle," he said, "I have promised Frances that I would—"

"Send her a note explaining you have been called away on business. She will understand."

"Me? Called away on business? She will not understand. When have I ever let business interfere with pleasure?"

Finian Chantry's eyes chilled. "If you do not wish to write the note, then do not do so. But I shall expect you to be riding west within the hour to overtake the stage for Pittsburgh.

"I wish you to see that the young lady in question, Echo Sackett by name, arrives safely at her home somewhere in the mountains east of Tuckalucky Cove, Tennessee.

"You are twenty years old, and—"

"At that age you were master of your own vessel. I know. You have told me the story a number of times since I was a child. Now—"

"If you are not in the saddle headed for Pittsburgh within the hour, and if the young lady in question does not arrive safely home, you may expect your allowance to be trimmed to six dollars per week."

Dorian started to speak, then looked again at his uncle. Finian Chantry, in this mood, was no one to argue with. "Six dollars a week? I would starve!"

"Many a good job pays no more than that. No, you would not starve, but you would have to find a job. You would have to go to work, which would be the best thing in the world for you."

Dorian Chantry studied the backs of his hands. Echo Sackett. . . . He had heard the Sackett story often enough to know what it meant to Uncle Finian, and what it had meant to his father as well.

"Where is she going from Pittsburgh? I mean, how will she go? By steamboat? By stage? How?"

"And where *is* Tuckalucky Cove? Is there such a place?"

"The Sacketts are backwoods people, mountain people. They have always preferred wild country. There's a town called Knoxville—"

"I've heard of it."

"Tuckalucky Cove is somewhere east of there, but whatever happens will probably happen before she reaches her mountains."

"Happens? You expect trouble?"

"Why else would I send you? And you had best take a brace of pistols and your rifle." Before Dorian could interrupt, he added, "Have you ever heard of Felix Horst?"

"His was one of the trials I attended when I first began studying for the law. Of course I remember him."

"I have reason to believe he is one of those who will attempt to rob Miss Sackett." Briefly then he explained about White and Horst, the will and the visit to White's office. Then he added, "Do not take this lightly. Horst is a first-class fighting man and he will kill without a qualm. I suspect others are involved."

Finian Chantry reached into his desk drawer and drew out a small sack of coins and tossed them on the desk. "Take that, for expenses. And you will find Archie waiting in the outer office."

"Archie? You mean the waiter from the club?"

"The same. Archie will go with you, but not as a servant, as a companion. He is a good horseman, and he's not a man to trifle with. I'd rather have him ride with you than anyone else I know. He went with me to the Dutchman's the other night."

Dorian stared. "You? At the Dutchman's? At your age?"

Finian Chantry smiled. "At my age. And I discovered I am still not as old as you might believe. In fact, I feel ten years younger for the experience." He stood up. "Go now, Dorian, and be careful. This is a deadly serious business."

Dorian pocketed the sack of money and after a quick handclasp went out.

The powerful black man, Archie, awaited him. "I have our horses at your quarters, sir, and I've packed what is necessary except for your weapons."

"You are armed?"

"Oh, yes, sir! I know Mr. Horst, and White as well, but unless I am mistaken, there will be others involved. White has a man working for him named Tim Oats, a very rough man, sir."

Dorian Chantry listened to the clop-clop of the carriage horse's hooves, his meeting with Frances only a dim memory. His uncle, Finian Chantry, was sending him out to protect a young lady from such as Felix Horst! Suddenly he was very proud. Uncle Finian must think well of him, after all, for this was no job for a child.

His thoughts skipped back a few years. He remembered the coolness of Felix Horst in the courtroom. Once their eyes had met across the crowded room. He still remembered the contempt in Horst's eyes, and flushed at the memory.

"If we ride hard, sir, we can overtake them at Chambersburg. It is a night stop for the stage, and they will start late the next morning."

"If nothing happens until then."

"There's a brief stop at Elizabeth Town, and then they cross the Susquehanna a bit later."

"What will Horst do?"

"I don't know, sir, but he will be careful. He is known to the law now and would get no sympathy from the courts. He will choose his time."

"Would he kill her?"

"Yes, sir. He would. He has killed before . . . and, sir? He knows the country we are going into. He used to operate along the Natchez Trace."

"What about Oats?"

"A thug, sir. A very strong man. He was a pugilist for

a time. He's been a gambler, a shoulder striker, a thoroughly bad man, sir."

"I've boxed some myself."

Archie glanced at him, then asked, "Have you ever fought, sir? I mean really fought?"

"I could handle them all at school. Don't worry. I can take care of myself."

"No doubt, sir, but the kind of fighting Tim Oats has done is not like you would do at college. It is quite different, sir."

Dorian was irritated. Of course it was different, but at school there had been some good fighters, and their training had been of the best. What chance would a common pugilist have against one of them? He said it aloud.

"Begging your pardon, sir, a man such as Oats would whip them all in one evening and never work up a sweat. There is no comparison between an amateur and a professional. And Oats is pretty good. I have seen him fight. I saw him go forty-two rounds with the Yorkshire Swiper."

"*Forty*-two rounds?"

The most he had ever done was five rounds—sparring sessions, at that. Sometimes they got pretty heated, but forty-two rounds? By London prize-ring rules a knock-down ended a round, although a fighter could be thrown down or could slip. Even so, forty-two rounds was a lot. It could scarcely be less than an hour, probably more.

Of course, there had been that fight he had with the hostler who was abusing a horse. How long did they fight? It must have been at least thirty minutes, and he had given the hostler, supposedly a tough man, a good beating.

They rode swiftly, clattering down lanes, thundering over bridges. At Elizabeth Town, only a few miles out, they made inquiries. Yes, such a girl had been aboard the stage.

Five-feet-two, reddish hair, cute as a button.

The description irritated him. "Cute" by whose standards? Harry Standish had raved about her when he came back to the table. "If they grow them like that in the mountains," he had said, "I've been living in the wrong place!" But then, Harry was easily impressed.

They changed horses in Middletown and rode swiftly on. Chambersburg was not far ahead.

At Chambersburg they arrived as the stage was loading. "No, sir," the driver said, "I ain't seen her since we pulled in. Seemed like somebody picked up her bag by mistake, and she went chasin' after them." He turned and pointed a finger. "Right up thataway. They turned the corner, and she after them."

"Who were they?"

"Little ol' lady and a burly, thickset man in a kind of checked coat. I remember he helped the ol' lady off the stage. I hadn't figured they were together until then. They rode separate."

Archie swore softly and glanced at Dorian. "They didn't wait no time at all, Mr. Chantry. They got her bag. They got her money, and maybe they've got her!"

"How long ago?" Dorian asked.

"Three, four hours. I called after her, but she kept a-goin'." He pointed. "She left that bag. She opened it, saw what was in it. Nothin' but some ol' carpet. Then she taken out like her skirts was afire!"

Angry and frightened for her, Dorian started up the street. Rounding the corner, he stopped, staring around. It was a long, narrow street with store buildings and barns empty of people. Dust swirled, then lay still.

"Let's move along slow," Archie suggested. "Maybe we'll find some clue. Maybe they ducked in some-where, maybe they kep' a-goin'."

Dorian Chantry pulled up and sat his saddle, survey-ing the street. "No use running after shadows," he suggested. "We have to think. Where were they going? Suppose they had it planned all along. By the time they got here, Miss Sackett would be tired. That's a long ride and she'd be bounced around a good deal, not much chance for rest. So she would be sleepy. I think they planned it that way.

"The old lady sitting beside Echo Sackett must have been a confederate. Oats was close to the door. He helped the old lady off the stage, taking the carpetbag from her. No doubt they hoped the switch would not be discovered.

"Suppose they figured it all out, Archie. If so, they would have to have a place to go, a place they could reach quickly and where they could stay out of sight until the stage was gone.

"Also, they may have planned what to do in the event the switch was discovered. In any case, they would need a place to hide. If she followed them, and we know she did, they knew it within a few minutes. She has not returned, so two possibilities are left. She is either still following them or she is their prisoner."

"Or she's been killed," Archie said. "It would be that or go to prison. Or maybe knock her on the head and leave her somewhere."

They walked their horses along the street. "She might leave some sign," Archie suggested.

"Why do that? She was alone."

"She's a Sackett. I've heard your uncle speak of them, and how they always hang together. Seems to me if a Sackett disappeared, somebody would come to find out how. She's got that uncle she spoke of to Mr. Finian, the one named Regal. She'd leave some sign for him. From what Mr. Finian said, those folks needed that money mighty bad. So I think she would leave some sign."

"If she could, and if she is still alive."

It was not something he liked to consider. Dorian found himself suddenly worried, thinking of a young girl in the hands of Tim Oats. Or of Horst.

Yet what sign could she leave?

They reached the end of the street without seeing

anything. Suddenly Archie pointed. "There's been a rig standing there! Look at the hoof prints. Must've stood here for an hour or more."

A buxom woman of perhaps fifty was sweeping the walk. Dorian walked his horse over to her.

"Ma'am?" He removed his hat. "Have you seen a rig? A horse and buggy, perhaps? I mean during the night? Or toward morning?"

"A rig, is it? Aye, that I did." She pointed. "I sleep by the window there, and his stomping and the creakin' of the buggy kept me awake the night long.

"Short of daybreak, though, two people came running up the street and got in, and off they went."

"*Two* people? You're sure there weren't three?"

"There was another one, a young lady like, but she came after, just as they were pulling away around the corner. She stopped, angry she was. She stamped her foot and said something . . . most emphatic it was."

"What then? Where did she go?"

"Yonder." She pointed toward a barn with a still-lighted lantern over the door. "She went yonder. It's a livery stable.

"Only a minute or two it was, and she was out of the stable and riding off after them. I don't know what was happening, but she was most upset, I can tell you that."

"Thank you, ma'am."

They sat their horses. "She's gone after them, then. We'd better catch them."

"Mister? You ask Pokey Joe at the livery. He can tell you about it. You tell him Martha Reardon sent you." She paused. "Is that girl going to get in trouble?"

"I'm afraid so, ma'am. I'm afraid so."

# 8

Gathering my skirts in one hand, I taken off up the street, but when I rounded the corner they were getting into a rig. This whole thing had been planned, and that team and buggy were just a-settin' there waitin' for them. As I rounded the corner, they got in and it taken off up the street.

Running after it would do no kind of good. A moment I stood there, my heart beating heavy. There went the money we so desperately needed—a mule to help with the farming, a new rifle for Regal, and some fixin's I'd had in mind for myself. All of it was gone because I'd gotten sleepy and didn't think to be suspicious of that little ol' lady.

She had gotten aboard to steal my carpetbag. That man in the houndstooth coat had seen the color of my bag when I got off the stage, so he knew what was needed to make a substitution. Had it been ladylike, I'd have done some cussin'. Then I glimpsed that lantern and the livery sign.

61

Luckily I'd put some of that gold in my pockets for the necessaries, so when I ran in there and asked for a horse, I slapped a gold piece in that man's hand before he had a chance to argue. Before he could say yes or no, I had me a horse out there and was slipping a bridle on him. That man caught fire and threw a saddle on him and cinched up. Saying I'd return the horse, I taken off after that carriage.

Chambersburg was a small city and they hadn't far to go to a country lane. I glimpsed them turn into it and followed on. Right then I was wishful for my rifle-gun, for with it I could have stopped that buggy before it got from sight. As it was, all I had was my pick and a short-barreled pistol which I carried along with a comb and perfume in my reticule, a sort of bag on long strings that hung from the wrist, usually. Womenfolks wore flimsy, gauzy clothes, all the fashion in the cities, that would not support a pocket, so the reticules were needful. The material of my traveling dress was of sturdier material, but the reticule was the fashion.

They were headed west and had a good lead on me, but I feared to ride too fast because they might turn off and I'd miss the turnoff in the dark. Moreover, they'd leave tracks for me to see when light came, and judging by the pale lemon color in the east, that would not be long.

There was no sort of plan in my rattled-up brain. I'd simply taken off after them. Surely he would have looked back and seen he was followed. It was likely he'd not be wishful to put up with that for long, so I'd best beware of a trap.

Murder, Finian Chantry had said. Murder was what Felix Horst had done, and would be prepared to do again, and so would this man up ahead.

The road taken led through the piny woods, or woods of some kind. It was too dark to make out. The trees crowded close to the sides and there were rail fences here and there. Suddenly, after we'd gone four or five miles, the trees fell away, leaving fenced pastures and fields on both sides, and far ahead, a light.

It was growing gray, but I could make out a cluster of buildings where the light was, and the buggy I was chasing pulled up and stopped.

I touched a spur to my horse and lit out on a dead run, hoping to catch up for a showdown, but the rig started off again and I saw somebody standing there, trying the door of the stage stop, trying to get in. When it did not open, she taken a quick look toward me and scuttled around the house, me after her.

She was coming up to the other corner when I reached out and grabbed. I caught me a handful of bonnet and gray hair that came loose in my hand, and the next thing I knew, that woman had turned on me, grabbed my wrist, and pulled me loose from my horse!

We went into the dust, me on top. She grabbed a handful of hair, and I'd never been that much of a lady. I slugged her in the nose with my fist, and when she tried to tear loose, her nose bleeding, I hit her again. And then I got up and looked at what I'd hit.

It was no little ol' lady at all, but a young, feisty woman with her makeup all scratched away and her hair pulled down around her ears. Her reticule had torn, and gold coins were spilled on the ground, two of them along with some other change. I taken up the coins. "Is this what they paid you to rob a poor girl? You ought to be ashamed!"

It was fresh new gold and I was sure it was mine. I put it in my reticule and caught up the reins of my horse.

"You taken all the money!" she protested. "I haven't enough for stage fare to town!"

"You have," I said. "There's some change, and it's enough. Anyway, the walk would do you good, give you a chance to contemplate on the error of sinful ways."

I fetched the horse closer and stepped into the saddle. "Where is he going?"

"None of your business!"

"Now, ma'am"—I spoke gentle, as Regal would have done—"you just tell me where he's goin' before I ride this horse right over you!"

She started to scramble up, and I bumped her with the horse, knocking her sprawling. She rolled over into a sitting position, her legs spread, hands behind her, bracing herself.

"You got one minute," I said. "Then I ride this horse right over you!"

She glared at me, then began to whimper. "He promised me forty dollars!" she protested. "That's a lot of money!"

"This here is a lot of horse," I said. "Where's he goin'?"

"I don't owe him nothin',", she said. "He's headed for a place in the Dickey Mountains. Used to be a hideout for Davy Lewis!"

Even in the mountains of Tennessee we'd heard of Davy Lewis, the Pennsylvania outlaw. He had been a counterfeiter at first, making false coin and passing it around, but after he escaped from jail, he'd become a highwayman of sorts.

Davy was said to be a sort of Robin Hood bandit who took from the rich to give to the poor. If he was like most of those Robin Hood bandits I'd heard tell of, the poor he gave to was himself or over the bar in the nearest tavern.

Now I could see the buggy track clear and plain. I got down from my horse and walked him a mite, studying the tracks of the horses pullin' that buggy. Horse tracks are like a body's signature, easy to recognize once you've seen 'em. I wanted to get these clear in my mind, and what was just as helpful, to know the length of their stride, so I could tell about where to look for tracks.

It was no doubt that Horst was mixed up in this, and the man up ahead was hand-in-glove with him.

The Doune pistol I carried held but one charge, and I'd powder and shot for but five more charges, but if I was close enough to shoot at all, I was not going to need more than one per man, and I was hopeful of doing no shooting at all.

One thing was on my mind. They had taken my money and I meant to have it back. Right then I wished it was Regal or my brother Ethan or anybody else but me. The trouble was, there was nobody else to do it, and if I called on the law, it would be too late. Unless I found some law close to where they were going, wherever that was!

There were farms along the way, mostly with rail fences and the houses built of logs, making me homesick for my hills. I rode swiftly now, watching the trail, picking up a hoofprint here or there that was clear and strong.

Where were they going? How far? Why did I think "they"? But of course, there was a driver—he who had waited with the rig? Felix Horst, perhaps? I did not know. I only knew that I could not return to home without the money we so desperately needed.

It was not that we were hungry, for the mountains provided game, herbs and nuts in season, sometimes fruit, and our planting provided vegetables and some grain. But there was so much else. My mother was growing old and I wished that she not have to work so hard. There were small comforts we needed. New bedding, new clothing, some of the small things to brighten our lives. We needed books, we needed something on which to build dreams. The money would change all that. Our decrepit old mule could be turned to pasture, our worn plowshare be replaced with another. It was little enough we wanted, but most of all I wished my mother to sit for a while in the sunset of her life, just to sit and live the sounds of our hills, the light and shadows upon them.

Until now I had just raced after them, but now I

began to think. What would I do? What could I do? There would be two men, and if one of them was Horst, he was a known murderer. Obviously they were leading me into the lonely hills. . . . What then?

My other pistol was in the carpetbag they had. It was fully charged and ready, and its barrel was full-length, not sawed off as this one was. Or had they already taken it from the bag?

I had one shot to fire; then I must reload.

Long practice with hunting had given me speed and skill, but no one could reload fast enough when facing a man with a gun.

So I must somehow meet them separately. I dared not chance a meeting with both at once.

"Echo," I told myself, "you got to be a good Injun. You got to be sly. You got to be careful. So hold back, stay on the trail, an' wait your chance."

Nobody knew where I was. To Finian Chantry I was on my way home. To Regal an' Ma I was either in Philadelphia or on my way home. Before either of them guessed anything was wrong, it would be all over.

Time and again I'd had to Injun up on wild game. I'd become like a ghost in the woods. It was that or go hungry. Now I would need all I'd learned. I thought back to stalking deer, getting so close I just could not miss. I'd never stalked a man before. It would be like cornering a catamount or a mean bear . . . only worse. The game I was stalking was used to being stalked, and it was smart.

My mouth felt dry and my heart was beating heavily. Was this what fear was? No, not yet. They were still ahead of me, but I'd have to ride wary. My feelin' was they would try nothing until they got away from cabins and places where folks might be. Then I'd have to ride slow.

"Regal! Regal!" I whispered to myself. "Tell me what to do! I got to do it, Regal, but I'm scared. I never figured I'd be scared, but I am. There's two of them, Regal!"

Twice I stopped at streams to drink. I was almighty hungry but I did not want to lose them, and it was coming onto dusk. I couldn't follow them after dark, so I'd best find someplace to hole up, maybe to get some grub.

The fields on either side were unplowed and looked abandoned, yet ahead of me I caught a glimpse of smoke—from somebody cooking supper, no doubt. I slowed my horse to a walk. This was careful time, this was the time they might lay out for me, waiting for a shot.

Twice, in small groves of trees, I drew up and studied the trail ahead, one hand in my reticule, holding that Doune pistol.

The Dounes were special guns, made in the last century by Scotsmen, and mine was among the last the Dounes ever made. They were the pistols the Scottish Highlanders loved, and many a clansman had been done to death by a bullet from a Doune pistol. John Murdoch had made the pistol I had, made it nigh onto fifty years before. Regal had cut four inches off the barrel for me to carry easy. The other one was my favorite, but a girl couldn't carry a pistol like that unless in mountain country.

Ahead of me the road curved. There were just two ruts for wagon wheels, with grass growing in between them. Some of the rails had fallen from the fences; everything looked abandoned or at least run-down. Drawing up again, I studied the layout ahead of me. Shadows were crowding from under the trees, and the trees themselves were losing themselves in the darkness. The twin ruts of the trail lay white before me, and there was a faint smell of wood smoke somewhere ahead.

My horse had his ears pricked. He smelled smoke, too, and knew it for a sign of folks. Maybe he could smell fresh hay or the barn. He seemed eager enough to go, but I held back, uneasy.

A trap—that was what I had to fear. Slowly I let my horse walk forward, my pistol ready, watching every clump of brush, every tree, alert for any sound of a horse or of a buggy wheel on gravel or whatever. I heard nothing.

Somewhere an owl hooted. My horse walked steadily forward. I was foolish to be apprehensive. Chances were they were miles away, and they were unlikely, I told myself, to try anything in the vicinity of a farm. Still, a body couldn't be too careful.

I was tired. I had been riding in the stage the night long and riding horseback all the day, and I'd had nothing to eat since around midday yesterday. I could still make out the buggy tracks, going straight on.

Now I could see lights in the cabin windows. I heard a door slam as somebody went in or out. Maybe I could get something to eat or even find a place to spend the night. I wouldn't be able to track the buggy tonight. Anyway, I could ask.

Another moment I glanced on up the road, but I could not see anything. It was too dark. Turning my horse into the gate, I rode up to the hitching post, and getting stiffly down, tied my horse, glancing back at the gate. They had forgotten to close it. Farm folks were careful about gates unless they were expecting somebody. Neighbors, maybe, or one of the family still out.

At the door, I rapped. For a moment, nothing happened. I could smell bacon frying and my stomach growled, a most ungenteel sound, but I *was* hungry.

I knocked again, and I heard feet approaching. The door opened, light fell across my face, sudden after the darkness. "Come in!" It was a man's voice. "Come right in! You're just in time for supper!"

Stepping in, I reached to close the door behind me, but it was already closing.

There was a candle on the table, a fire in the fireplace, and there was bacon in the frying pan, and a smell of coffee.

"Come right in and set! You're just in time to have supper!"

The door closed behind me, a bar fell in place. There were two men, and one of them was the untidy young man from Mr. White's office; the other was the man in the houndstooth coat.

# 9

For a moment I just stood there. The younger man was at the fire with a fork in his hand. The man in the houndstooth coat had moved between me and the door. There was no way I was going to get past him and get that bar moved and the door opened before they stopped me.

"Thank you," I said. "Travelin' makes a body mighty hungry. The smell of that bacon stopped me."

Me bein' casual like that kind of stopped them in their tracks. They didn't know what to make of me and I hoped to keep it thataway. I was trying to let them think I didn't know who they were or that they didn't belong here. I could see now this had been an abandoned house. I should have guessed it from the weed-grown fields and the fences with rails down.

"Mind if I set down? It's been a long day." Keepin' my face bland as I could, I reached out a hand. "My name is Sackett, Echo Sackett. I'm bound for Tennessee.

Should be meetin' my Uncle Regal in Pittsburgh. He's comin' on to meet me."

I was lyin' in my teeth, but I was wishful they would think I was expected somewhere and if I didn't show up folks would be makin' inquiries.

"Finian Chantry, he's an old friend of my grandpa, he sent word to Regal to meet me. Didn't like me travelin' alone."

I kept on runnin' off at the mouth, afraid trouble would start when I stopped. Also, I was hopeful of worrying them some. If they thought there'd be folks lookin' for me or tryin' to find what had become of me, they might hesitate to do whatever they'd had in mind.

"Regal, he's one of the greatest trackers and Injun fighters in Tennessee. He wanted to come with me, but couldn't get away in time. Be good to see him again."

I drew a breath, but before anybody could speak, I said, "My stars! That bacon sure does smell good!"

"Give her some bacon and bread." The broad-shouldered man took off his hard gray hat and put it on a stand nearby. He had a thick neck and one crinkly ear, and somebody, sometime, had broken his nose.

"Thank you, sir." I sat down and primly smoothed my dress. "I didn't catch your name, sir?"

"Timothy Oats," he said grudgingly, "an' that there is Elmer."

"We met." Elmer put a plate of food before me, his eyes leering. "We met before."

"Oh? Oh, yes! You're that nice young man from Mr. White's office! Somehow I thought you were a city man. I didn't expect to find you away out in the country like this."

"Gimme some of that coffee," Oats said.

Did they know I was chasing them? Had they seen me run around the corner after them? I had to chance it.

"I left the stage in Chambersburg," I said. "It was too rough. The ride, I mean. I left my things on the stage, but I hired a horse. It's easier riding, and I thought I'd stop and see some friends."

"Friends? You said you was from Tennessee," Elmer protested.

"I am. From Tuckalucky Cove, or thereabouts, but we've friends up thisaway." I grasped at a name. "I should say a friend. He's a hunter. Known all over this part of the country. Name of John McHenry."

"Never heard of him," Elmer said.

"If you was a hunter you would. He's a dead shot. He's fed himself and his folks for years. He may hunt for the market, too. I don't know about that."

"What's so great about huntin'?" Elmer demanded.

"If we didn't shoot our meat, we wouldn't have any. I reckon it is the same in these mountains up here. We have great respect for a man's shootin' ability. Take us Sacketts, for example. All of us are hunters, and we are all good shots. Right now," I said, "we've got a feud goin', too. With the Higginses, but we're ahead of them right now. Our boys shoot better than they do."

"What about the law?"

"Folks don't bother much, as long as we only shoot each other. I guess the law figures sooner or later we'll wipe each other out, but that'll take a while. Must be forty Sacketts in the hills now, and some down in the flat country. If you step on one Sackett's toes, they all come running."

The plate before me was empty. Now came the big gamble. I drained my coffee cup and pushed back my chair. "I got to get goin'. If I don't show up pretty soon, those McHenry folks will be huntin' me."

I started toward the door, then stopped, brushed an old piece of sacking away, sacking that had covered my carpetbag. "An' I'll just take this along with me." When I straightened up, the bag was held in my left hand. In my right I had that Scottish Highlander pistol.

Oats had started to rise; Elmer had turned, startled by my sudden switch.

"You just set still. This here pistol shoots mighty straight, an' I wouldn't want one of you boys to have to bury the other. Just set real quiet, now."

I put down the bag, pushed the bar away, never taking my eyes from them, and picked up the bag. Elmer was getting over his shock and he put the fryin' pan down real gentle. I don't know what was in his mind but didn't aim to be around to find out.

Oats had kind of leaned forward, starin' at me, and suddenly he came off that chair with a lunge.

Stepping quickly back, I managed with the tip of a finger on my gun hand to start the door swinging shut. He hit it with a bang and I ran for my horse. I heard him cursing, heard Elmer yell something; then the door jerked open and they both came tumbling out. I was in the saddle, trying to hold the carpetbag and reins with the same hand, ready to shoot if need be.

Then I was out of the gate and headed down the road. Somebody behind me was swearing, and they were running for the barn. It was going to take them time to hitch up, and meanwhile, I was off and away.

Lucky? You bet I was lucky! When I got up from the table, my only thought was to get away from them; then I saw that carpetbag only partly hidden by the sacking. I just acted without thinking. Only thing saved me was, my action was unexpected. They figured me for a woman who would set quiet and do their bidding. Growin' up as I had, I was active as any boy and ready for anything.

I taken off down the road. Ahead of me I could see a ridge, black against the sky. Next thing I knew, I was slowing down for a cluster of houses. Two of them seemed to be taverns, but closed for the night. This was Loudon, or some such place. Cove Mountain was ahead of me, and a winding road up it. Slowing down, I started up at a walk, a twisting trail toward the top. By now they would be after me, and they weren't the kind of men to think of their horses. Nonetheless, I taken it easy.

It taken me most of two hours to reach the crest, although I doubt if it was more than seven or eight miles. By the time I was topping out on the ridge I could hear them coming.

Near the top of the hill was another tavern. There were some wagons about, loaded with household goods. Movers, I suspected. Two men were standing in the road arguing, and from their voices they must be Irish.

They turned when they heard me coming, and I pulled up. "Paddy," I said, "would y' be doin' me a favor, then?"

"It's a lass, Rory! Would y' believe it in the night? A lass!"

"There be two men followin' me, thieves they are, and I just got free of them. I'd not want you to get hurt, but if you could stop them? Hold them up for a bit so I can get away?"

Rory stood straight, as if on dress parade. "I would, ma'am! I shall stop them or know the reason why. Do they come now?"

"Right behind me. Two men in a buggy, and one of them is a fighter, I think."

"Who's a fighter?" The other Irish thrust himself forward. "It's a bit of a fighter I am, too! We'll stop them, ma'am, an' go a round or two whilst we wait. We'll see if he's a fighter or not!"

"Thank you, sirs! You are gentlemen indeed!"

Now I remembered my father speaking of this place, for all along the mountains the story was told of battles between the settlers and the redcoats several years before the Revolution. Two forts, one at Loudon and another at Bedford, had been taken from the British soldiers, and there had been many a fight with Indians in those days.

Ahead of me was a village called McConnell's Town, and beyond it another of those steep ridges like the one I'd just come over. The man from whom I had hired the horse had told me I might leave it here at a place called

Noble's Tavern, although whether Noble still kept it, I did not know. The food there was good, he had said, explaining it all very rapidly as he bridled my horse. And the tavern was a stage stop.

Unless the stage had passed me when I had stopped at the cabin, it was still behind, and with luck I could resume my passage.

Tired I was when Noble's Tavern appeared, and a man came out to take my horse. "You have ridden far," he said. "I know this horse."

"I'm to leave him with you. Has the stage come?"

"It hasn't, but it is due within the hour." He was a kindly man, and he saw the tiredness of me. "Go inside," he said. "The missus will put something on for you."

She was a cheerful lady with red cheeks and a brusque, friendly manner. "Oh, you poor dear!" She pointed. "Go there, you can refresh yourself. When you come out, I shall have breakfast for you."

The breakfast was good—sausage, eggs, ham, and some applesauce she had made herself. There was no one about, so she sat with me, very curious, as I could see.

"I've come a far piece, and I am going to Pittsburgh, but there's two men coming along after me." I described them. "They have tried to rob me, although it is little enough that I have. They will be coming along soon."

"Don't you worry! We'll have none of that about here!"

She got up as I was finishing my meal. "Come! You're dead tired! You come back to my room and lie down for a bit. Bring your things. You rest up, and when the stage comes, I'll not let them leave without you."

Alone in her room, I sat down on the bed, opening my carpetbag. Nothing was disturbed and the other Doune pistol was there, and more powder and balls. To be sure, I recharged the pistol, for there might have been dampness in the powder. Then I lay back on the bed and slept.

Dreaming, I was. Dreaming of a tall young man with broad shoulders but no face to him—only my feeling that he was handsome. He was riding a horse and he was looking for me. It was a nice dream and I was sorry to awaken, but it was a voice I heard, a voice beyond the wall.

"Cut my lip, he did. I'll say that for the bugger. He was game. I put him down three times, and each time he came up swinging."

It was Timothy Oats speaking, and then I heard the other one, Elmer. "But you whipped him, whipped him good. What I don't understand is why he challenged you, a stranger."

Oats's voice was low and ugly. "You're a fool! Can't you see? It was that girl. She put him up to it. Just wait! Wait until I get my hands on her!"

There was a rap on their door. "Come! Come, now, gentlemen! You must be off! We've the stage coming in and must serve them who've only a minute or two!"

"Have you seen a young girl? On a bay horse?"

"A girl? At this hour? You must be daft! We've only just opened the doors! If anybody passed, it must have been in the dark! Be off with you now, we're busy folk here. We've no time for drunken brawlers."

"Now, see here! I wasn't drunk! I—"

"Whatever, we've only food enough for the stage, so be off with you now. If it is breakfast you're wanting, there's another tavern down the road a bit. No doubt whoever you were looking for would have stopped there, for they show a light the night long."

Up, I was, and slipping on my boots. When I had bathed my face and arms, with no time for more, I combed out my hair. It was a sight, and I was a sight.

A brush here and a touch there, however, and I felt better and may have looked better. I was straightening my clothes a bit when she came to the door.

"Come! There's fresh coffee and you can have a bit before the stage comes." She put a cup and saucer on the red-checked cloth and poured coffee. "There were two men just here, one with his knuckles all skinned and a bad welt on his cheekbone, as well as a split lip. Were they the ones?"

"I heard them talking. It was an Irishman at Loudon who fought him."

"Ah, that would be Rory! What a lad! And a brawny good lad, too, if he did not nurse the bottle so much! Always ready for a fight, he is, and all for the sport of it. There's no meanness in him!"

She bustled off and I sipped the coffee, thinking. Timothy Oats and Elmer were somewhere ahead of me, and they would try to catch me. If not on the road, then in Pittsburgh.

It was unlikely they would expect me on the stage, for they would be sure I had gone on ahead of them. I was finishing my coffee when the stage rolled in, but only three people came to eat. Three and the driver.

He looked at me, startled. "You, is it? Well, you've still your fare paid to Pittsburgh, so get aboard." He glanced down at my bag. "Did you get yours back? Or is this the other?"

"It is mine," I said.

"We're changing horses, but will be off in a minute."

Before he could go to the kitchen, where he was headed, I stopped him and explained about the attempt to steal my carpetbag and the two men on the road before us.

"If they hail you," I pleaded, "do not stop for them. They'll just be looking to see if I am aboard."

"Rest easy," he said. "I'll be stopping for nothing if I can help it, although it is a slow climb up Sidelong Hill, and a narrow road."

With so few people traveling, I put my carpetbag on the seat beside me, where I could rest an elbow on it and where my second pistol was close. I opened the

neck of my reticule a mite to have an easier grasp on
the pistol there.

People got into the stage. I leaned my head back
against the seat and closed my eyes. A whip cracked
and we went off with a lunge, rumbling over the rough
road, headed for the mountains again.

I was very tired.

# 10

In Pittsburgh I stopped at the same rooming-and-boarding house as on my way east, and Mrs. O'Brien had a fine large room for me in the old house where she lived. Her maid brought a tub and hot water to my room and I bathed, washed my hair, and meanwhile she did the best she could with my traveling dress. It came back to me looking like new.

No steamboat was leaving that day or the next, so I made inquiries. Mrs. O'Brien suggested I go by way of Wheeling and save some miles of travel. I said nothing to her about Timothy Oats or Elmer.

Yet she was puzzled by me, for after breakfast I remained in the parlor, looking frequently out of the windows to see if the place was watched. It was unlikely they would find me so soon, but I dared take no chances.

"What is it, Miss Sackett? Whom do you watch for?"

For a moment I hesitated, then explained that two men had tried to rob me, and I feared they had followed me. Nevertheless, I must be about my business, and the sooner I returned to my hills, the better.

"If you wish to go by way of Wheeling," she suggested, "there is a coach leaving from an office on Water Street. It is a new line, but they have several stages."

"They will be watching the stages," I said, "and the steamboats too, I am afraid."

A thought came to me. "Coming here, I saw a number of wagons bunched in some vacant lots."

"Movers." Mrs. O'Brien's tone was disparaging.

"We all were movers at one time, Mrs. O'Brien," I said. "Even you when you left Ireland."

"I suppose so, but somehow it seems different."

"Settled folks always look down upon the unsettled," I said, "but somebody has to open the new lands. When they are settled in their homes, they will feel just as you do." A thought came to mind. "I am going down and look them over."

"Please! Be careful! A young girl like you! And you have to walk right past Mr. John Irwin's ropewalk. There are some mighty rough men thereabouts."

"I shall be all right."

Despite the smoke of the factories, which often hung low over the town, Pittsburgh had a beautiful site. I walked along, my reticule hanging from my shoulder to an inch below my hand.

At the ropewalk, men were busy making ropes, and although some of them glanced my way, they did not speak. One young man close to the street tipped his cap to me, and I bowed slightly to acknowledge it but did not smile or meet his eyes.

Beyond were at least two dozen wagons drawn up, where some children were running about, playing. A woman was hanging out her wash, several clothespins in her mouth. She looked very neat despite the work she was doing, and the two children playing nearby were clean and bright-looking.

I stopped. "Ma'am? May I speak with you a moment?"

She took the pins from her mouth and made a quick gesture to straighten her hair. "Why, of course. What can I do for you?"

"You are traveling. Would you by any chance be going toward Wheeling?"

"As a matter of fact, we are going that way."

"Ma'am, I want to go to Wheeling, and I can pay you a little." Before she could suggest it, I said, "I do not want to take the stage." Adding, "Some men are following me."

"It is very crowded, but—"

"I'm a mountain girl," I said. "I'm used to making do. I'll sit wherever you put me, and I'll help with the cooking. I'll tell stories to the youngsters—"

"Here comes Ralph, my husband. We will ask him."

He was a strongly-built man of about thirty-five, a man with a strong, determined look about him, but there was kindness, too.

"As far as Wheeling? Yes, we can take you." He had given me a quick, searching look. "It will cost you nothing, but if you could help with the children . . . ?"

"I'll help, but I will pay, too," I said. "I will give you three dollars, and two more when we arrive."

"That's too much," he said. Then he grinned. "But we'll take it. Lord knows, living is expensive. I had hoped to find a job here but have had no luck, and it is too expensive to live here.

"Why, a simple room would cost me one hundred dollars for the year! One hundred dollars! Can you imagine? And beef is seven cents the pound . . . even cornmeal is a dollar the bushel! I can't afford to stay on."

He glanced at me again. "We have no comforts, you know. It is just wagon travel, and we are loaded."

"She says she is a mountain girl, Ralph. She may be used to roughing it."

"Oh, I am! You need not worry about me. I shall try to disturb nothing and keep out of the way. One thing I ask. Don't mention the fact that I am going with you, and I shall join you before daybreak."

He looked at me again. "These men who are following you. What do they look like?"

My description was brief, but enough, I know. He nodded. "You'll not worry," he said. "You can stay inside the while, or get out and walk when you wish. I doubt if they will expect you to take that road."

Mrs. O'Brien was drinking coffee when I came into the kitchen. She gave me a quick look. "There's nobody about. I just looked. Drink your coffee. I've some soup heating up, so you can have a bit before you go."

"I'll just have time. You've been very kind."

"Think nothing of it. Just be careful."

Dark it was, and still. I donned my poke bonnet and peeked from the window. No light showed. It was very dark. Taking the bag in my left hand, I loosened the knot on the reticule and let my fingers grip the Doune pistol.

The room behind me was dark, and Mrs. O'Brien opened the door very quietly. "Go now, and the good Lord with you!"

A floorboard in the porch squeaked, and I stood very still, surveying all that was about me. Nothing moved. The air was damp from the river and there was a smell of wet cinders in the air. Tiptoeing down the steps, I started at once. It was three long city blocks to where the wagon waited. The first block was houses, all dark and still at this hour; the second was the ropewalk and a lumberyard with a stable adjoining; then the open area where the wagons waited.

It was going to be all right. I let go of the pistol and walked swiftly, gathering my skirts, not to let them rustle too much, for I wished to hear any small sound. The reticule dangled from my shoulder again. My carpetbag was heavy. I switched hands with it, but after a half-block, as I came up to the ropewalk, I changed hands again.

Far ahead of me I could see a faint glow from what must be a lantern. Ralph, harnessing his horses, no doubt. The shadows worried me. A body simply could not see—

The movement caught my ears too late. Rough hands seized me, and there was bad breath in my face. "Don't you scream, or I'll kill you sure. Now, you just listen to me.

"Tim is across the town watching at the stage station. You just be a good little girl, and I'll not tell him I found you."

He spoke softly. "I don't know where you figure on goin' this time of night, but I know what we can do, you an' me. We'll just—"

Lifting a boot, I stamped down hard on his instep and at the same time smashed back with my head into his face. He was taller than me, but my skull caught him on the chin and he let go, staggering back. Swinging the reticule by its strings, and it carrying my pistol, some shot, and a few coins, I caught him alongside the head. Small I may be, but I've worked hard my life through and am strong. The swinging reticule laid him out in the dust, pretty as you please. He groaned once, started to rise, then fell back. A moment I looked at him, not in the least sorry for him; then I went down and joined them at the wagon.

Several wagons were all ready to pull out, and Ralph said never a word, just motioned to the back of the wagon, and I climbed in and we were rolling.

Among the piled-up packages and rolls of bedding, I found a place to settle my back in a niche, and soon fell asleep, awakening to find it daylight and to see two round-eyed children staring at me.

"Well!" I said cheerfully enough. "My name is Echo, what's yours?"

The little girl looked away, twisting her fingers, but the boy said, "Jimmy. I am Jimmy Drennan, and this is my sister, Empily. She's scared."

"Empily?" I asked.

"Emily!" she said sharply. "*Empily!* He always calls me that!" Then she looked at me. "Is Echo a name?"

"It's my name," I said, "but, yes, it is a name. We use it for the echoing sounds we hear, but it was a name before that. Echo was the name of a nymph, a sort of sprite, I guess you'd say. She was always chattering, so Hera, who was a goddess, ruled that she should never speak first, and never be silent when anyone else spoke. But Echo fell in love with Narcissus, and when he died she pined away until only her voice was left."

"That's just a story!" Jimmy said.

"You're right, it is, but a very, very old story. When I first went to school, my teacher told me all that."

"Are you going to pine away until you are just a voice?" Jimmy asked.

"Probably not," I admitted. "I have never met Narcissus."

"You will," their mother said. She sat up. "I am Laura Drennan. I hope they aren't annoying you."

"You know they aren't. We don't have any young-uns where I live, and I miss them."

"Where is your home?"

"In the mountains of Tennessee. Away back in the hills. We have lots of bears back there."

"Do they eat people?" Jimmy demanded.

"Not often," I said, "although I suppose if they got really hungry, they might."

"You've *seen* a bear? A wild bear? Up close?"

"Several of them. In fact, my uncle is laid up right

now because of a fight he had with one. He was without
his gun and he disturbed a bear that turned on
him."

Ralph Drennan looked over his shoulder. "You mean
he fought a bear? Without a gun?"

"He had a knife and later a double-bit ax." She
glanced at Jimmy. "That's an ax with two blades. He
had to fight with what he had, but he killed the bear."

Ralph glanced at me, unbelieving, then turned back
to his driving. There was silence in the wagon. Jimmy
was the first to speak. "Did the bear bite him?"

"Several times. He clawed him pretty bad, too. Regal
killed the bear, then dragged himself almost home. We
found him by the spring when we went for water."

By midday we were winding along a very rough road
through a dense forest, the trees so thick overhead
that it was shadowed and still. Ours was the lead
wagon, but Ralph Drennan's team was a good one and
they moved steadily on, bumping over logs, squeezing
past fallen trees, stopping occasionally to give the horses
a breather.

His rifle lay in a corner of the wagon, and it looked to
be almost new. I could not see the make of it, but it
was a Lancaster rifle, I was sure of that.

"Do you hunt much?" I asked.

He looked over his shoulder. "I have hunted scarcely
at all. Not since I was a boy. I have been working in the
city," he added, "and decided there was little future for
me there, so we decided to try pioneering. We are
going to Kentucky," he said, "and probably to Missouri."

We moved on again, and I fell asleep. When I awakened again it was almost dark and the children were
asleep; moving carefully, I worked my way to the front
of the wagon.

"Want me to spell you?" I asked.

"You can drive a team?" He was amazed.

"Where I come from, ever'body drives," I said. "I
can drive, I can plow, I can do what's necessary."

"I'd gladly let you," he admitted, "because I am tired, but I've got to find a place to camp."

"Better do it soon," I suggested, "or it will be too dark to see where we're at. Why don't you catch a nap? I can find a camp."

He hesitated. "Well, I'll rest just for a minute."

I taken the reins and he moved back into the wagon. Glancing up through the trees, I could see he'd already waited too late if a body was to gather firewood and such, so I kept my eyes open. Sure enough, we hadn't gone two miles when I saw a small clearing near a branch, a small stream that rustled over the rocks, heading for the Ohio and the sea.

Rounding the wagon against the woods on the far side, I brought the team to a halt and showed the other wagons where to turn in. There were just three others, and there was room enough, but barely. Catching a glimpse of some open space, I walked that way and found a small meadow. Others had stopped here before us. Unhitching the team, with Jimmy to help, I led the horses out on the meadow and picketed them there. The others, following me, did likewise.

Laura got down from the wagon with Emily. "Better keep them close," I advised. "Young-uns get lost in the woods an' might never be found."

Taken me only a minute or two to break some sticks, gather some shreds of old bark, and get a fire going. It is surely amazing how a fire cheers folks up. "I'd better wake Ralph up," Laura suggested.

"Wait until we've coffee made," I said. "He's put in a long day."

The others built another fire and we made do between the two. Coffee was boiling when Ralph got down from the wagon. "I'm afraid I just passed out," he said. "I'm sorry."

"No need," I said.

He came up to the fire and Laura poured him a cup of coffee.

"Maybe," I said, "come daybreak you'd let me use that rifle of yours? This here's game country, and I might get us some meat."

"You can shoot?"

"A mite," I said. "I can try."

# 11

Come daybreak, I taken that rifle and started off across the meadow. The trees were almighty big, poplars fifteen, sixteen feet around, and red maple almost as big. The soil underfoot was as good as any I'd seen, hundreds of years of leaves falling, decaying, and turning to earth, and big trees struck down by age, wind, or lightning also were decaying and adding to the richness of the soil. This Ohio country was a mighty fine land. Easing through the woods beyond the meadow, I saw another clearing right ahead, and a deer standing there, not more than eighty yards off.

These folks didn't have much, and we needed the meat, so I fetched him with a neck shot and taken the venison back to camp.

Ralph looked up, surprised. "You got a deer?"

"Small buck," I said. Then I looked at him. "I aim to pay my way." I handed back the rifle. "Take good care of it, that's a fine weapon. I'll clean it when we get rolling."

We shared the meat with the other wagons, giving each enough for a meal.

It was slow going there at first, but we hit some open stretches that enabled us to make time. All the time, I kept my eyes ready for Timothy Oats and Elmer. They would be coming along behind, or maybe even waiting for me in Wheeling, where I figured to catch the steamboat.

On the third day I killed four ducks in four shots. Jimmy was with me and he carried two of the ducks back to the wagon. "That's good shooting," Ralph admitted. "You were lucky to catch them sitting."

"She didn't," Jimmy said proudly. "They took off from the water and she got one that time. She got the others later, shot 'em on the wing."

"Flying ducks? With a rifle?"

"Back to home," I said, "I never had no shotgun there at first. It was shoot 'em with a rifle or forget it."

Back in the wagon, we sang songs, some of them hymns which we all knew, others the songs we'd learned as youngsters or those they sang in the mountains. Often in the hills folks would put new words to old tunes, or pick up a refrain and work something around it. We sang what songs we had, and made up others as we went along.

Wheeling was built on a bottom along the river, most of the town on one street, with a hill rising behind it. Here, too, there was a ropewalk, some stores, warehouses, and an inn where I found a place to stay the night. There would be a steamboat in the morning, and I'd made up my mind to leave it at Cincinnati and travel across country to home.

When they put me down in front of the inn, I said good-bye to Laura, Ralph, and the youngsters, and I guess we all cried a little bit, sorry to part, with small chance of ever meeting again.

The food was good at the inn, and I waited by the window, watching out for Timothy Oats and Elmer.

There was no sign of them, nor was there when I went down to the boat.

I'd recharged my pistols and was ready for whatever. In a shop near the inn I'd found a seamstress who had a sky-blue dress and bonnet that taken my eye, so I bought it. My gray travelin' dress was lookin' kind of used up. I also bought from her a travelin' outfit, somewhat cheaper, but sturdy. I had the feeling I'd need it.

With my carpetbag stuffed, I stood by waitin' for that boat.

They might be aboard, but I was going to ride it anyway. If they were eager to fetch trouble, I'd not let them yearn for it.

So I was standin' there on the dock when I heard that ol' whistle blow and saw that steamboat come chug-chuggin' up to the island.

I looked up as it came alongside, and there by the rail were two men standin', a big black man and a tall, right handsome fellow with as fine a set of shoulders as I'd ever seen. My heart did a flip-flop. *It couldn't be!* Not *here!*

Suddenly I was glad I'd bought that blue dress and the bonnet with the lace, but he wasn't even *looking* at me! He didn't even see me!

A man tipped his hat. "Ma'am? Were you going aboard, ma'am?"

"Oh? Oh, yes! Of course!"

"Better hurry, ma'am, that gangway is down only for minutes. The cap'n, ma'am, he's in a powerful hurry!"

Taking up my bag, I went to the gangway. Glancing up there again, I saw the black man watching me. He said something to the tall young man, but he was looking off over my head at somebody. I turned around, and there behind me was Elmer.

He grinned at me, showing his ugly teeth. "Carry your bag, ma'am?"

I turned away from him and went up the gangway, and as I came aboard, Timothy Oats was standing there,

# FLINT
## IF HE HAD TO DIE, AT LEAST IT WOULD BE ON HIS TERMS..

### Get a taste of the *true* West, beginning with the tale of *FLINT* FREE for 15 Days

Hunted by a relentless hired gun in the lava fields of New Mexico, Flint *"settled down to a duel of wits that might last for weeks...Surprisingly, he found himself filled with zest for the coming trial...So began the strange duel that was to end in the death of one man, perhaps two."*

If gripping frontier adventures capture your imagination, welcome to The Louis L'Amour Collection! It's a handsome, hardcover series of thrilling sagas by the world's foremost Western authority and author.

Each novel in The Collection is a true-to-life portrait of the Old West, depicted with gritty realism and striking detail. Each is enduringly bound in rich, Sierra-brown leatherette, with padded covers and gold-embossed titles. And each may be examined and enjoyed for 15 days. FREE. You are never under any obligation; so mail the card at right today.

### Now in handsome Heritage Editions

Each matching 6" x 9" volume in The Collection is bound in rich Sierra-brown leatherette, with padded covers and embossed gold title... creating an enduring family library of distinction.

SILVER CANYON LOUIS L'AMOUR

THE DAYBREAKERS LOUIS L'AMOUR

FLINT LOUIS L'AMOUR

not smiling or anything, but just looking at me. His cut
lip had healed but there was meanness in his eyes. I
walked right past him and went along the deck to an
officer.

He was a young, handsome boy with cornsilk hair
and a face red from the sun. "Cabin, ma'am? Come, an'
I'll show you."

"Sir? That man by the gangway. I think his name is
Oats. I don't want my cabin close to his. Please?"

"I'll see, ma'am. I am afraid there's little choice,
we're that crowded, but you need have no fear aboard
this boat, the cap'n is a stickler for propriety. You will
not be disturbed, I promise you."

The cabin was very small and there were two bunks;
a valise was already sitting on the lower one.

"Oh? I must share the cabin with someone?"

"Yes, ma'am. Most folks sleep out on the deck, we're
that short of space. Seems like everybody's travelin'
these days. You goin' far, ma'am?"

"To Cincinnati, I think. I might go further."

"Hope you do." He touched his cap to me. "It isn't
often we have a girl aboard as pretty as you."

"Thank you. Do you know who is sharing this cabin
with me?"

"Yes, ma'am. She's an older lady. She's going to
Cincinnati too. She is called Mrs. Buchanan."

"Called? Isn't that her name?"

He glanced around quickly. "I wouldn't repeat this,
ma'am, but I was on another steamboat where she was
a passenger, and she had a different name then."
Suddenly he was worried. "I shouldn't have said that,
but you be careful. You see, I could be wrong about
her."

When he was gone, I looked up at that upper bunk.
My carpetbag was heavy. How ever was I to get it up
there? And I did want it where I could feel it near me.
I'd lost it once and did not intend to again.

It was heavy, but I managed, after all. I put it on the

back side of the bunk, and my pillow covered it a mite. From down below, I couldn't see it at all.

At the mirror, which was not a very good one, I primped a little, tucking in a curl here, fluffing my hair a little there. Then, letting my bonnet hang by its ribbon, I went out on deck. There was a place nearby where I could stand by the rail and still keep my cabin door in view.

We were already out from shore and moving down the Ohio.

The banks were high bluffs and heavily wooded. Here, as on the roads, were a lot of people moving. They were in flatboats or keel boats, once in a while somebody in a canoe. Most of them were going downstream.

A voice sounded close by, and I looked around. There was that young man! The black man was beside him. He glanced at me, and I smiled.

He stared, shocked, then turned away, turning his back on me. It was him, all right, those same broad shoulders and the back of his head I would know anywhere.

Well! If he wanted to be that way, all *right*! Glancing toward my cabin, I saw a woman at the door. She was folding a parasol and about to enter, so I crossed to the door and went in behind her.

Hearing my step, she turned. She had large, very blue eyes, and lips so red they had to be painted, but the job was well done and one could not be sure, not really.

"Oh? You are the young lady who shares the cabin?"

"I am."

"You're very pretty, you know. Do come in! It is crowded, but we can manage." She held out her hand. She wore several rings. Two of them looked like diamonds, although I had never seen a diamond, just heard of them. "I am Essie Buchanan. I am going to Cincinnati."

"So am I."

"Oh? Perhaps I can entertain you there. It is a rough town, but a good, lively one. If you like a good time, it is the place to have it. No end to the men, and most of them very handsome."

"I shan't be there long."

"That's too bad." She glanced at me again, a quick, measuring look. "You are traveling alone?"

"I am." I paused. "I think I'm to be met."

She talked a little, mostly of clothes and the weather, and after a bit she started back to the deck. "Would you like to join me? On the promenade?"

"No, thank you. I think I will just rest."

When she was gone, the cabin smelled of her perfume. I didn't like it very much. She was a handsome woman, and very expensively dressed, but something about her didn't seem right. Or maybe what the young officer had said was influencing me. I must not be prejudiced. Nonetheless, I had to watch the cabin. Timothy Oats would steal my bag and all that was in it if given a chance.

A thought occurred to me. What was Dorian Chantry doing *here*? This was a long way from the hunts, balls, and belles of Philadelphia. Maybe I was mistaken. After all, I had never seen his face. I could not be sure. He must think me brazen, smiling at him like that. The thought made me flush with shame. What a fool I was!

If I had not seen him, he certainly had not seen me, his back to me and all.

The young officer who had shown me to my stateroom explained the boat to me. Although I'd heard most of it before, I listened with rapt attention. Long ago, Regal advised me: "Men like to talk of what concerns them. Learn to listen, and if you can ask a question now and again, do it. Give them those big eyes of yours and you'll have no problem. You'll be bored often enough, but you'll learn a lot, too, and they will go away telling everybody what a charmin' girl you are.

"You learn to listen, or at least act like you're

listenin', and you'll find menfolks doin' all sorts of things for you. Smooths the way, y' know? An' if you're modest about it an' don't flaunt yourself around, the women will like you too.

"A man, he's got to get along mostly with hard work an' persistence, but with a woman it is mostly maneuver. Men have to maneuver too, especially so when it comes to womenfolks."

"You see," the young officer was saying, "there's two lines of cabins, with the main cabin in between. The doors from the cabins open on the main cabin, where folks can mingle and get acquainted. We serve meals there, too.

"Most of the cargo is stowed on the main deck, but sometimes bales of cotton or whatever are piled higher than the deck we're on."

His name was Robinson and he seemed a nice young man. "If there is anything I can do for you, just call on me."

At supper in the main cabin there were three tables. Sure enough, I was seated at the same table with that tall young man. The captain introduced everybody to everybody else, and sure enough, he was Dorian Chantry. When my name was mentioned, he looked across the table and our eyes met. He flushed and looked away, which seemed odd, for he was supposed to be a ladies' man.

There was an older man at the table, a stocky man, taking on some fat at the belt, with thinning white hair, but a face that seemed young for the hair. He glanced at me when my name was mentioned, but said nothing. His name was Ginery Wooster.

At the third table, Timothy Oats was seated close to Essie Buchanan. They were talking. I did not look at them, not wanting them to realize I'd noticed. I had to get away; I had to get off this boat, somehow, some way.

Suddenly I felt trapped, closed in. I did not trust that

woman, and now she was talking to Oats. Probably it
was idle conversation, but I dared not risk it.

I glanced across the table at Dorian Chantry. Did I
dare ask his help? Did he even know about me?

If I could just get off, in the middle of the night,
when no one suspected. . . .

I was a fool to be thinking of him. He had not so
much as noticed me. It was my family I must consider,
and what this money would do for them. We had been
poor for such a long time. We lived all right because we
could hunt, but now it could be different.

Very different.

What I needed now was time to think, to plan. If I
could get off this steamboat now, or soon, I could get a
horse and ride south. It was closer to home than
Cincinnati, although wilder country, I believed.

If I only had a map of the river! Often the steamboat
stopped at small places, sometimes only landings. If I
could get off without anybody knowing, get off in the
middle of the night. . . .

That nice young man, Robinson. He would know. He
had offered to help.

He wasn't thinking of that kind of help, I warned
myself. Still, if I could just get off somewhere. . . .

I could get Mr. Robinson to show me a chart of the
river. I knew they must have some in the pilothouse.

Suddenly I was startled from my thinking. He was
speaking to me. Dorian Chantry was speaking to *me*!

# 12

"Did I understand you to say, Miss Sackett, that you are leaving the steamer at Cincinnati?"

"That is my present plan, Mister . . . is it Chantry?"

"Dorian Chantry, at your service. I believe you know my Uncle Finian?"

"I've had the pleasure, and indeed it was a pleasure. He is a very fine man, a remarkable man."

"And a stern one, very stern."

"With reason, perhaps?"

His glance was cool. "No doubt he feels it so." He resumed the former topic. "From Cincinnati you go home, I believe? Is not that very rough country?"

"Some might think it is."

"But there is a stage? Or can you take another steamer?"

"There is, I think, but right across country is quicker."

He was irritated. How foolish of her to come so far, unprotected and alone! Because of it he had to leave everything and come on this wild-goose chase, escorting a girl who did not seem in the least grateful. She was pert, almost impudent.

"I am astonished that your family would permit it. Suppose you met a bear? Or a man of evil intention?"

I made my eyes very wide. "I'd take him home for supper."

"What? You'd invite such a man to your home?"

"I meant the bear." I smiled innocently. "Could I do less?"

His expression showed his exasperation. "Uncle Finian said I was to see you safely home. He was quite worried about you. He said there were—"

"They are here."

Startled, he looked up. "*Here?*"

Before he could say more, I said, "It is very nice of your Uncle Finian to worry about me, but I shall be quite all right. I would not want you to go to so much trouble. There are bears where I am going, and quite a few men, but most of them are very nice."

"It is preposterous for you to travel alone." He glanced at the woman who sat beside me. "Don't you agree?"

"I should say I do! And across country? Dear me!"

"But there was no one else. My uncle was not well, and the trip must be made. Anyway, it is nearly over now. Soon I shall be home."

Irritated, he looked down at his plate. What must he think of me? Yet I could not keep from teasing him. He looked so exasperated, and so handsome.

"You must not worry, sir. I shall be all right, and there will be no need of an escort. I shall manage very nicely."

He was very cool. "I am not at all sure of that. From what I have heard, you have had your bag stolen from you already—"

"I have it back."

"And you disappeared from the stage for several days. I had no end of trouble finding you."

I gave him my prettiest smile. "But you *did* find me!

I can't thank you enough! I don't know what I'd have done without you!"

He gave me a very cool, level glance. "Miss Sackett, my uncle insisted I see that you got home safely. I shall do my best to do just that."

I glanced at the third table. Timothy Oats was gone. Essie Buchanan was rising. Where was Elmer?

From where I sat, I could see the door to my cabin, but of course, there was an outer door, too. It was locked, I had made sure of that, but such men know how to open locks as simple as that would be. "If you will excuse me . . . ?" I pushed back my chair and arose.

Dorian Chantry got to his feet also. "Will I see you at breakfast, Miss Sackett?"

He was certainly tall. "I believe so. Thank you, Mr. Chantry."

As I walked away, I heard the woman who had sat beside me say, "She's very pretty, you know." I did not hear his reply, if he made one, although I very much wanted to.

Our cabin was empty when I reached it, my carpetbag untampered with. I turned and looked at myself in the mirror. That blue dress *was* becoming.

I shook my head. I must stop thinking such thoughts. What I must do now is get home with the money. It would do so much for us, make my mother's years so much more comfortable. As for Regal, he was probably recovering very well, but how did we know? Several men who had been clawed or chewed by bears had never really gotten well. A man I knew at the store said it was because bears often fed on half-decayed meat and fragments of it clung to their teeth. Regal should have a doctor look at his wounds, and if I got home with the money, we could afford it.

One side of me did not want Dorian Chantry along at all, but another side certainly did want him to come with me. I knew the woods where we would soon be. I knew how to move like an Indian, but did he? Suppose he got chewed by a bear? I'd never forgive myself.

I had wanted to meet him, and now I had, but I must have left him with a very bad impression. It was obvious that he disapproved of me and that I was a nuisance. Surely he had other plans. He had not wanted to come all the way out here into what was almost a wilderness, just to be sure some silly girl got home safely, somebody who should not be out there alone anyway.

The more I thought of it, the worse I felt. My pretty blue dress! It must seem very plain and dull to someone who saw so many beautifully gowned women, and saw them all the time.

How could I even talk to him? What did women like that talk about? And what did they talk about to a *man*?

Essie Buchanan came in and stepped into the corner where the washbasin and mirror were. She began fluffing her hair, and glanced at me out of the corners of her eyes. "You shouldn't be back here," she said. "It is much too early! I met a couple of interesting men out there, and I told one of them about you. He would like to meet you. I told him I would try to arrange it."

"No, thanks, I need the sleep. I've been traveling a lot."

"You'll never meet any men back here. They don't permit men aft of the mid-ship gangway, you know. Come on! We'll have some fun."

"You go ahead."

"That man I mentioned. He's middle-aged but he's worth a lot of money. To the right girl he'd be very generous."

Well, I just looked at her. Regal had told me about women like her. "No, thanks," I repeated.

After she had gone forward, I lay staring up at the underside of the deck above me and thinking. It was unlikely that either Elmer or Timothy Oats would attempt anything while aboard the steamer, although they would be watching for their chance. It was when I went ashore that I must move with care. What I must think of was some way to slip away from them. It was then I thought of the Big Sandy.

But that was Indian country, hunting ground for a half-dozen tribes; the Creek, Cherokee, Shawnee, and several others hunted there. I was known to the Cherokee, and the Sacketts were known to them all, I suspected, but I'd be taking a great chance. Still, it was early in the season and hunting parties would not be out in any number.

On the lower Big Sandy there were some fine farms, and a body might even get a horse, or if not that, a canoe. I could make my way up the Levisa Fork into Kentucky, cut across the toe of Virginia, and be right back in my own mountains in no time.

There were Sacketts on the Clinch River, a bunch of rowdy boys but good folks and cousins of ours. If Timothy Oats followed me into Clinch Mountain country, one of those big Sacketts was liable to bounce him up and down all the way back to the Ohio.

First thing tomorrow I had to lay hold of Robinson, that young officer. He could get me a map or at least a layout of the river so's I could see what to do.

In the mountains we work from sunup to sundown, so when day broke I was up, moving very quiet so's not to disturb Essie Buchanan or whatever her name was. I eased out of the room and walked forward to where I could look down the river and feel the wind in my face. It was mighty nice. I had not done much traveling, but if a body had the time, it was a way to live. I could see us chugging away downstream with high bluffs covered with trees and here and there an occasional cabin or farm. I could see those across the river better than on the nearer bluff because they were so high. Then I remembered how Pa had been on the Ohio close to the Mississippi when the New Madrid earthquake hit. He had told me that bluffs like this, a hundred and sometimes two hundred yards of it, would cave off into the river. It must have been a sight.

That earthquake even had the Mississippi flowing back upstream for a while, tilted the whole bottom of the river for miles! Just as I was fixing to go back to the main cabin for breakfast, young Robinson found me.

"A map? A chart, you mean. I guess I could draw one for you."

"Just so I would know where I am on the river," I suggested. "I could pay you for it," I added.

He blushed. "Pay me? I'd enjoy doing it for you," he said. "I really would. I'm proud you thought to ask me."

"I just thought you would know," I said, "you studying to be a pilot and all. If anybody would know the river, you would. Just as far as Cincinnati," I suggested. Then I added, "Do we stop at night? I mean to let folks get on or to take on freight?"

"Sometimes, and sometimes we tie up at night. They do that a lot on the Mississippi and Missouri because of the snags and sawyers in the river that can tear a boat's bottom out. You have to be able to see."

Dorian Chantry was at breakfast, and that surprised me some because I had an idea easterners didn't get up all that early. His hair was combed with a kind of wave in it and he looked neat as if he'd stepped out of a bandbox, as Pa used to say.

"Well? Good morning, Miss Sackett! I hope you slept well?"

"I did, and a good morning to you, sir!"

There were only a few people in the main cabin and nobody at the same table with us. He glanced around, then asked, "Last night you suggested those men who tried to get your money were aboard here?"

"They are," I said, "but stay clear of them. They are rough men."

He stiffened a little. "I can be rough if need be."

"If you have trouble with them, it will be," I warned.

"What happened back there? I mean when you lost your bag?"

So I told him a little. I surely did not tell him all, but how I didn't even suspect that little ol' lady and how she switched bags on me and was getting away with Oats when I taken after them.

"By the time I got my bag away from them, I'd gone on down the road a ways, so I caught the stage when it caught up." There was no need·to tell him about the house by the road or how I got my bag back. "The stage, I mean."

"They did not follow you then?"

"They did, but I got away from them." He needed a warning, so I said, "There was an Irishman who said he would stop them. He was a big, strong lad, too, but he did not do it. Oats had a couple of bruises on him and some skinned knuckles, was all."

"I see."

Well, now he knew what he was in for. Dorian Chantry was a fine, strong young man but I could not see him in a country brawl with Timothy Oats. Dorian could fight the gentleman's way, not the eye-gouging way of the riverboat men or such as Oats.

"Look," I said suddenly, "why don't you go back and tell your Uncle Finian I am all right? I shall be safe enough once I am into the mountains. I am a Sackett, after all, and Sacketts and rough country are as twins. I shall be all right."

"He sent me to look after you."

"You're a handsome lad," I said honestly. "I'd not see you hurt."

"Hurt? *Me?* I shall be all right. No," he said then, "I shall see you all the way home to your cove."

"You'll have to get some other clothes," I warned. "In the brush those you're wearin' won't last at all. You need linsey-woolsey or deerskin."

We ate our breakfast then, not talking much, and other folks began to come in and out. Something about me was a worry to him, I could see that. I was not like the girls he'd known, nor could I talk to him as they might have. I was used to talking with men and boys, used to saying what I meant and no two ways about it.

He was more the gentleman than anybody I'd ever met, knowing all the ways of them, and it was mighty fine, being treated like a lady, like you were something special. All the boys I knew treated me like one of them—I mean, not as if I was special. Although they were respectful enough, it just wasn't their way.

"Mr. Chantry," I said, "that Timothy Oats has something in mind. He means to have that carpetbag from me and I've got to outguess him. If I let him do as he's planned, he'll win, I know he will. Pa used to say, and Regal says the same, that a boy should never play the other man's game. If I stay on this steamboat I will be playing their game, and I think he's got a wheel turning with that Essie Buchanan, who shares my cabin. They've been talking, and—"

"I was going to speak to you about that," he said then. "You should not be sharing a cabin with a woman like that. It's a disgrace."

"It won't be for long," I said.

"It has been too long already. I shall speak to the captain."

"Don't you do it." I had looked up to see a man come into the main cabin. I saw him look around and I saw his eyes meet mine.

"We've troubles enough," I said. "There's Felix Horst!"

# 13

For a minute or two I just sat there. Timothy Oats and Elmer did not worry me much, but Felix Horst was something different. I was afraid of him.

A body could see at a glance this was not only an evil man but a wily one. I would never have tricked him as I had Oats, nor would he have bothered to fight with that young Irishman. He would simply have killed him and chased after me, wasting no time. He wanted that money I carried, and meant to have it.

Oats had no doubt gotten Essie Buchanan to keep an eye on me, so if I got away, I had to slip away from her.

"Mr. Chantry," I said, "you have to help me. I am going to leave the steamer. I am going to get away. You can help me."

"How?" He was cautious, not trusting me or my ideas.

"You've got to ask me out to take a walk on the deck after supper. I mean"—I blushed a mite—"like you were courting me."

He studied me coolly. "And then what?"

"I slip off the boat. I get ashore and take off up the Big Sandy. I figure I can rent a horse or buy one. Or maybe a mule. Then I head for home."

"Not without me."

"Are you up to it? That there's rough country, Mr. Chantry. It won't be like riding to hounds. You'll be sky-hootin' it along ridges, dippin' down into hollows, you'll be pushin' through woods and brush and maybe have a mite of Injun trouble."

"*Indians?* What you are talking about isn't exactly the far west!"

"No, sir, but there's Indians. The Cherokee mostly know us Sacketts. Some of the others do, by reputation. The ones that know the Sackett name won't do us harm, but there's Shawnee around, too, and they aren't friendly with the Cherokee right now. The Creek, too, sort of go their own way."

I tried my coffee and it was still hot. "Have you got a rifle, Mr. Chantry?"

"A rifle? No, of course not. Not here."

"You'll need one, and so will I. I left mine at a tavern on the way, but it is some little distance. Regal an' Ma, they convinced me young ladies in Philadelphia do not carry rifles as a reg'lar thing."

"Can you actually shoot a rifle? You're serious?"

"Yes, sir, I have shot a rifle."

He did not take that seriously, I could see. In his world womenfolks danced, rode to hounds, partied around, and wore pretty clothes most of the time. Well, that was all right, but in the mountains things weren't quite like that.

"Mr. Chantry," I said after a bit, "we should smile more, like we were enjoying each other's company. Let Horst and them think something's going on betwixt us. If we act too serious, they are apt to get suspicious."

He smiled beautifully.

"There! That's better! A body would think you'd never courted a girl before."

"I am not exactly courting you, Miss Sackett. If you wish to deceive them, of course—"

"We've got to. We can't let them guess we're going to duck off this boat and head upcountry. I've got a map coming to me. A young officer promised he'd find one for me, or draw it."

"A young officer?" He raised an eyebrow. "You do get acquainted, Miss Sackett."

"Yes, sir, when it's necessary. He's a right handsome lad, too."

"You've talked to him?"

"Of course. Several times. He's the tall blond officer."

"I haven't noticed," he replied somewhat sharply.

"No reason why you should. You noticed Essie Buchanan, though, didn't you?"

"She intends to be noticed. She dresses to draw attention."

"And she gets it." I swallowed some coffee and then added, "She wanted me to meet some men. One of them, she said was very well-off."

"You didn't accept, I hope?"

"Well, no. But a girl has to think of her future, and most of the boys back in the hills are spoke for. You see, I am sixteen, and where I come from, that's almost an old maid."

"As I have said, I do not think Essie Buchanan is fit company for a young girl." He glanced at me in a very professorial manner. "She's what is known as a shady lady."

"Well, what do you know? I always wondered what one of them would look like. Regal's told me a good bit about them."

"And who is Regal?"

"I thought I told you about him. He's my uncle, and he goes round and about from time to time and is quite a man with the ladies. Right now he's laid up. Had him a little go-around with a bear."

"You mean he shot a bear?"

"Not exactly. This was a notorious bear, a trouble-making bear, and he tackled Regal, not knowin' he was a Sackett, so Regal had to kill him. Not until they'd disputed the subject, however."

"Killed him? How?"

"Mostly with a knife. He's got him one of those Tinker knives and he cut that bear up considerable. Finally did him in with his ax but not until the bear chawed on his leg and arm and clawed his ribs."

"You mean he killed a full-grown bear with a hunting knife and an ax?"

"Wasn't no other way. The bear wouldn't wait for him to fetch his shootin' iron, so they just had at it, an' Regal fetched him."

She looked at him seriously. "You ever eat much bear meat, Mr. Chantry? Grandma Sackett, she says there's no other way to raise a boy. Got to feed 'em bear meat when they're young. Ever' two, three days she'd take down her rifle-gun and fetch home a bear from the woods. Got so we had to move."

"Move? Why?"

"No more bears. She either killed 'em all or they just got tired of dodging her and taken off out of the country. Grandma, she was a caution.

"If you do come to the mountains with me, we'll feed you some bear meat. Good for you. Puts hair on your chest, Regal says."

He looked shocked. Maybe I shouldn't have said anything about hair on his chest. Young ladies didn't talk that way, I guess. No doubt where he lived young ladies weren't supposed to know that a man grew hair on his chest.

"I got to go now. I have to meet that young ship's officer. He should have that map for me."

He stood up, his features stern with disapproval. "I could have gotten a map for you," he protested.

"Here? On this boat? A chart of the bends and of the places they will stop?"

Walking forward to the rail which was just above the steps leading down to the cargo deck, I waited, watching the river. Suppose there was no stop? Could we leave the steamboat while it was moving? We would need a boat, of course, or a raft.

Robinson came along shortly. He *was* good-looking in his uniform coat and cap. He glanced around to see if we were watched, but there was nobody in sight.

"Here's the Big Sandy, right after we make the bend, after passing the Guyundat. The Indian Guyundat is a creek on the right side." He gave me a sharp look. "What d' you want to know all this for?"

"Mr. Robinson, you must tell nobody. *Nobody*, do you understand? I have to leave the boat and I do not want anyone to know.

"Mrs. Buchanan will certainly be asking. Tell her I've gone forward, tell her anything, but try to make her believe I am still aboard."

"But, ma'am, there's nothing there at Big Sandy! I mean, there's a landing. We'll nose into the bank there and load some freight, but it won't be more than five minutes."

"That's all I need. But please! Don't tell anyone! Not even the captain!"

"Somebody will see you."

"Maybe, maybe not. I hope not."

He had drawn a dark line on paper showing the river and where the various creeks came into it. I studied it for a few minutes after he was gone, and then returned to my cabin. Essie Buchanan was not there, so I looked through the carpetbag to make sure everything was all right. I did not know what they intended, but suspected they planned to rob me when I left the boat in Cincinnati.

Our arrival at Big Sandy would be very late. If I could I would smuggle the carpetbag out of the cabin when Essie had gone to supper, passing it through the outer door to Dorian Chantry.

What did the arrival of Felix Horst mean? Had he received some knowledge that the others had failed? But how could he know that?

No, Horst must have some plan of his own. Perhaps he wanted me to be far enough away from Philadelphia or Pittsburgh and in a place where it would take time for word to get back, if it ever did. People were often lost on the river, and the Cave-in-the-Rock had been a hideout for outlaws for years.

Horst was no fool and he would not want to risk being taken by the law again. He would know how much money I was carrying and he would choose his time very carefully.

The day passed slowly. Green Bottom Ripple, a dangerous place, was negotiated with care. I watched the creeks to check them off in my mind; then I went back to my cabin and lay down on my berth. I wanted to rest before the coming night.

Essie Buchanan came in. "What's the matter, dearie? Not feeling well?"

"I've a headache," I lied, "Just not feeling well, I guess, or maybe it's ague. I've had fever an' chills all the morning. I think I'll just lie here."

"Want me to bring you something?"

"No, thanks. I'll just rest."

At suppertime I went to the main cabin, and as Essie was at another table and could not observe, ate well enough. Dorian Chantry sat across from me.

There were folks sitting close by, so we could not talk of what we planned, nor about ourselves. There was time to look around and see those who traveled with us. One was an Englishman, interested in western America, who wanted to know everything. He asked a sight of questions and it seemed like he was suspicious of answers. He evidently had a different idea in his mind than what he was discovering to be true, and was uneasy about it.

He was surprised to find so many people reading Dickens, Scott, Thackeray, and the lot, although I don't know why. A lot of western folks were readers, and books were precious things, hard to come by and much treasured.

"Miss Sackett? Do you read? I mean for pleasure?"

"Of course."

"You have books in your home?"

"Mighty few. Pa used to lend books, and somehow they never seemed to come back. My Uncle Regal, he took to Scott. When I was no bigger than a button he was always reciting *Lochinvar* or something from *Marmion*."

"From memory?"

"Of course. We Sacketts all have good memories. Part of it comes natural, part of it is from learning. When folks don't have many books, they have to learn their history by heart. We learned the way ancient people did, like the bards of the Irish or the Welsh.

"It is a good deal like traveling across country. A body lines up on a peak or a tree or something in the way of a landmark, then as he walks, he checks the backtrail, which always looks different. We learn to pick out a tree here, a rock there, or something of the sort to guide us. Once seen, we don't forget it.

"Pa, he started teaching us that when we were youngsters, as his pa did before him. It was the same with history or the folks in our family. We learn about the principal Sackett of a time, and all the folks connected to him. You mention any one of the family back three, four hundred years and we can tell you who he or she was married to and what happened to their get. Their children, that is."

"I never heard of such a thing!"

"You mention Barnabas, now. He was the first of us in this country, and any Sackett can tell you what ship he crossed on, who his friends were, where he settled, and how."

"It must have been some such means that was used by the druids."

My eyes were wide and innocent. "I suspect so." I purposely sounded vague. I had talked as much about that as I was going to.

Dorian asked me many questions, and I noticed he was listening carefully. From time to time he glanced at me curiously, as if wondering about some of my answers. Ginery Wooster was setting back in his chair, seeming to pay us no mind, but he was listening, too.

"We all remember that way, after a fashion," I said. "Somebody says 'George Washington,' and right away you think of Mount Vernon, of 1776, of John Adams and Thomas Jefferson, Valley Forge and all that, and each one of those things tips you off to another set of memories.

"Well, we just extended that, a-purpose. We didn't just kind of do it by happenstance. We sort of extended it out further and further, and as youngsters we were taught not just to learn something but to learn something else that went with it. Pa, he used to say that no memory is ever alone, it's at the end of a trail of memories, a dozen trails that each have their own associations.

"There's nothing very remarkable about it, or even unusual except that, like I said, we do it a-purpose."

"But there must be limits!"

"Maybe, we just never found one yet."

Dorian, he pushed back his chair and got up. "Miss Sackett? There are many lights in the sky. Can you come and tell me their names?"

"Well," I said, "I can start you off right. That big round white one is called the moon. Does that help any?"

# 14

Bright was the moon upon the narrow waters, black and silent the shores except for the occasional lights from a settler's cabin, blinking feebly from the trees or some meadowed bluff. There was no sound but for the chugging of the engines, yet we were not alone upon the deck, for others had come from the main cabin to enjoy the night.

Essie Buchanan was there, accompanied by a heavyset man with muttonchop whiskers. Was she watching me?

"I had not realized the Ohio was so large a river," Dorian said aloud, but under his breath he whispered, "I wish they'd all go to bed!"

"We must wait them out," I said, not at all unhappy about it. Then I added, "The step to the bow is right behind us."

"Archie will be down there waiting for us," he said softly. "He has your carpetbag hidden there." After a

112

moment he said, "I still believe we should stay aboard until Cincinnati."

"They are waiting for us there," I said. "If we move now, there will be fewer of them. We may even get away unseen."

"If there's trouble," Dorian said, "stay out of it. Leave it to Archie and me."

"Maybe I could help."

"You? You're just a girl. What could you do in a fight?"

"Probably not very much," I agreed meekly, "but I could try."

"Stay out of it. I do not want you hurt." Then he took the fun out of it by adding, "Uncle Finian would never let me hear the last of it."

There was a rustle of water about the bow, the low murmur of others' voices.

"Are you going into law like your Uncle Finian?"

He shrugged a shoulder. "I haven't decided. I've thought of raising horses. I like the country life."

"You will see some beautiful country in the next few days. Not the best of Kentucky, but some of it. If you wish to raise horses, there's no better place to go."

"Maryland," he objected, "Maryland or Virginia. Who would wish to be out in this wilderness?"

"But it isn't wild anymore. Only in the mountains."

He turned his back to the rail and rested his elbows on it so he could see what the others were doing. "But some of the people even live in log cabins!" he protested.

"I live in one. I love it."

He was astonished. "You? In this day and age?"

"My grandfather built our cabin. It was the third one built on the spot or close to it. The first two were burned by Indians during the War of the Revolution."

"A log cabin? In 1840?"

"It is warm and snug and we have a beautiful view of the mountains."

He glanced at her face in the moonlight and the slight glow from the main cabin windows. She *was* pretty. But living in a log cabin? In these modern times?

"We have a log barn, too, and we churn our own butter, bake our own bread. Mostly we make do with what the land provides, barrin' a few things from the pack peddler, like needles an' such."

"But don't you ever want to get away? Don't you think of leaving? Coming to the city?"

"Oh, yes! I've thought of it, and talked of it, too, with Regal. Only we Sacketts have lived in the mountains for quite a spell.

"You've got to wake up of a mornin' with the clouds lyin' low in the valleys between the mountains, the tops of the peaks like islands. You've got to see the mountains when the rhododendrons are all abloom, or the azaleas or mountain laurel. We don't have much in worldly goods, but we're rich in what the Lord provides."

"Have your family always stayed in the mountains?"

"No, I reckon not. There was Jubal Sackett, a long, long time back. He taken off to the west, crossin' the Mississippi. He returned once, but when he left the second time, it was reckoned he'd never come back. Jubal had the Gift."

"The 'Gift'?"

"Second sight. He often knew things before they happened."

"I don't believe in that."

"Some don't. I never had the Gift, but it runs in our family."

"It's superstition."

"I reckon so, but it has played a big part in our family story." Glancing around, I whispered, "They are going in."

"But we shall have to wait. From the sketch you showed me, it must be some distance yet."

"An hour or more, with the current." I hesitated, then added, "When the stage is lowered, we must go ashore at once, before anybody will think to watch."

"We'd be better off to wait for Cincinnati," he protested. "We will be better off where there are people."

No use telling him I wasn't used to people caring for me. Where I came from, a body took care of himself and did not look to other folks for protection or even help. If it came, and among mountain folks it often did, then you accepted it and returned the favor when you had the chance, only you did not look for it or expect it.

Once we got ashore along the Big Sandy, I could make myself mighty hard to find. Out there where the forest brushes the sky, that's my kind of country.

Something stirred in the shadows and I put my hand on his sleeve. Surprised, he looked down. I was standing very close, and I liked it. "There's somebody there," I whispered, "near the ladder from the Texas deck."

Maybe we had done all the wrong things, waiting out there until everybody else turned in. Being wishful of standing in the moonlight with him, I'd forgotten they might not wait for Cincinnati or anywhere. We were here, in the night and alone, and they were coming for us.

"I hope you can fight," I whispered. "We've got it to do."

They were between us and the main cabin, which would be empty at this hour. We were closer to the steps leading down to the main deck, where cargo was stowed. Minute by minute we were drawing closer to the Big Sandy. There was no way we could get off now without them knowing, but I had an idea they just intended to kill us both and throw us into the river.

They came out of the shadows, and there were not three of them, but five. They moved toward us, moving in a sort of half circle. None of them looked familiar. Horst must have hired himself some thugs.

Dorian Chantry spoke, and I must say he was cool enough. "Come, Miss Sackett, we must be going in. I promised the captain I would speak to him before I turned in."

He took me by the elbow, but I withdrew it from his hand. Not that I did not like it, but I wanted my hands free for what was coming.

I'll give him this. He did not stand waiting for invitations. Suddenly they rushed, and he stepped to meet them. He struck hard with a left and a right, and the man he hit went down.

A big sweaty, smelly man grabbed at me. "Now, little lady . . .!"

Two of them were swinging on Dorian and time was a-wasting. As that big man grabbed at me, I slid that pistol from my reticule and eared back the hammer.

He heard the click and seemed to catch himself in mid-stride. I let the hammer fall, there was an explosion, and that big man taken a quick, staggering step back, then fell against the rail.

Somebody, somewhere up on the Texas yelled, "What was *that*?"

There was a sound of running feet, and almost at once the attack broke off and those men just scattered.

"Was that a shot?" Dorian grabbed my arm as I slid the pistol back into the reticule. "Are you hurt?"

"Let's get away from here," I said.

The steamer was nosing in to the bank and I could hear men down below getting the rigging away to lower the stage. Swiftly we went down the ladder. The man Dorian had hit was struggling to get up; the man I'd shot was just lying there. People were coming from the main cabin as we disappeared down the steps to the bow.

As the stage lowered into place, we ran ashore. A big

deckhand called out, "Hey? You folks! You can't go ashore here!"

By that time we were in the shadows of a shed, and I heard Dorian's friend Archie whisper, "This way, *quick*!"

There was a landing, a shed, and a road leading back into the country. We got into the darkness under some big old trees and stopped there, catching our breath.

There was confusion on the landing. Cargo had been waiting and there had been some heavy boxes waiting to be off-loaded.

I heard somebody call out that a man had been shot.

"Thug," somebody else said. "What's he doing on this deck? He's no passenger!"

"I think we had better move," Archie whispered. "The further we get, the better."

Glancing back, I could see, in the light from the stage, a tall man wearing a planter's hat. He was looking off our way, although I knew he could not see us. It was Horst. There was a cluster of houses and barns, then a land that led away along the Big Sandy. As we moved away, the sounds from the Ohio receded. We stopped a couple of times to look and listen.

Had we gotten away? I was not at all sure. Felix Horst was no fool, and he wanted the money I had.

Nobody had much to say, walking that muddy road up the Big Sandy, climbing a mite, passing a farm here or there. Dogs barked at us but nobody came to the doors, and it was graying sky before we fetched to a halt under a big old sycamore. One limb of it, big as the trunk itself, ran parallel to the ground and we sat on it, resting our feet.

"Maybe we could get horses," Dorian suggested.

"A canoe," I commented, "then we could take off up toward the forks of the creek."

"That man back yonder?" Archie wondered. "Who could have shot him? One of his own crowd, maybe?"

"He didn't seem to be dead," Dorian commented. "I

saw him trying to roll over when we went down the ladder."

Me, I hadn't any comment to make. My only worry was getting loaded again, and I was hopeful of recharging my pistol alone, where they could not see. No use them getting ideas, but it was my shot that broke the attack, coming unexpected like that, and alarming folks in the cabins.

"There's a farmhouse," Dorian suggested, "smoke coming from the chimney. We might buy some breakfast."

"I'm for that," Archie agreed.

"All right," I said, "but we'd best not linger over coffee. We will have followers comin' up the trail after us, and they won't be bare-handed. They'll come to fetch trouble this time."

We walked down to the lane and spoke to the shepherd dog who came charging at us. I put a hand out to him and after a moment he sniffed it, then seemed to accept us, although he barked again from time to time as we come nigh the door.

That door opened and there was a man standing there who had to put his head outside to stand up, he was that tall. He had thin reddish hair and a large Adam's apple.

"We're travelin' folks," I said to him, "headin' back for my own mountains, and these gentlemen are keepin' the bears off my back whilst we walk. Right now we're shy of breakfast."

"Come in an' set. Ma's puttin' on some sidemeat an' corn fritters. Coffee's a-bilin'. This here is fresh ground from our own parch. Never did take to lettin' anybody else parch m' coffee."

He glanced at Archie, who had seated himself on the steps where he could watch the road.

"He belong to you?"

"He's a free man. Has never been any other way."

"Then I'd warn him to get back across the Ohio. Some who come huntin' escaped slaves aren't pa'tic'lar who they lay hold of."

"I'll tell him. He's a good man."

"If he's keepin' watch for you all, tell him to set in the barn window. That way he can see a mile or two down the road." He paused, glancing from me to Dorian. "You two runnin' off?"

Dorian was embarrassed. "No, sir. Miss Sackett had business with my uncle and he wanted Archie and me to see she got home all right, to Tennessee. She's been followed by some bad people."

We ate, taking our time. I described Felix Horst, Tim Oats, and Elmer. "There's others, but those three are the ones we know."

"Your name is Sackett?"

"It is."

"You got kinfolk in the Clinch Mountains? Seems to me I've heard tell of Sacketts down thataway."

"Some. They're cousins, sort of."

I carried food to Archie. "We'd best be movin', ma'am." He glanced at me. "You know how we're goin'?"

"Up the Sandy. If we could find a canoe, we'd move a lot easier."

Dorian was up and ready. The sandy-haired man was watching him. "You need you a rifle-gun," he said. "If those follerin' you have a rifle-gun, they'll pick you off."

"Do you have one to sell?"

The man shook his head. "I've my own, but we can't live without meat, and I shoot my meat. You might find one of the McCoys with an extry rifle-gun, although folks hereabouts only has what they need, mostly."

"We'd better go." Dorian held out his hand to the man, who accepted it. We thanked his wife and waved at the children and went out by the gate.

"They're comin'," Archie said, "a mile or two back. At least one of them has a rifle."

That scared me. If that one could shoot, there would

be places he could lay his rifle-gun on a rest and take out any one of us at a distance.

The trail followed the Big Sandy. We crossed a meadow wet with morning dew and went into the trees. It was shadowed there, and still. Dorian led the way, and he had a considerable stride.

There was a place where the trail curved out from the woods to the bluffs above the river. We looked back and glimpsed them, five of them.

"They're gainin' on us," Archie said. "We've got to make our fight."

# 15

"Not yet," I said, and they looked at me, surprised, I guess, that a girl would speak up at such a time. "We'll make ourselves hard to catch," I said. "Come on!"

My eyes had been busy and I'd seen a dim trail taking off through the trees. As I started, Dorian hung back. "Where's that go?" he demanded.

"We'll find out, won't we?"

Muttering, he followed. The trail led down through the trees into a wooded hollow. There were deer tracks, but I saw no human tracks. Swiftly I led the way through the trees, past some craggy rocks, and across a small stream. Waiting there, I waved them past and then tried to make the signs of their passing less obvious. Oats was a city man, I was sure, and I suspected Elmer was. I knew nothing of Horst, but if I could confuse them a mite, it would save time.

They had walked on, as I meant them to do, and I stood listening. There was no sound but a faint stirring of wind, and then I heard a voice, somebody calling.

They had already reached the place where we'd turned
off, but had they noticed? I was hoping they would
continue on along the Big Sandy.

Regal had hunted down this way a long time back,
following an old trail left by Pa in his younger days, and
I was hopeful of finding the trail that ran parallel to
Blaine Creek, or sort of.

A moment more lent to obscuring tracks, and then I
followed along after Dorian and Archie.

It was quiet in the woods, but sound carried when a
body was in the open. I must caution them about
talking. From time to time the trail emerged on the
banks of the creek or in a meadow, but we moved on,
heading south. Every step was drawing us closer to
Sackett country, but we still had a ways to go. If I only
had my rifle-gun!

It was back yonder, waiting for me in a tavern where
I'd left it, and far from here. Yet, I dearly wanted that
rifle and I studied in my mind to find a way to get there
and pick it up. The tavern was miles away to the west
and south, but mostly south.

When I fetched up with Dorian and Archie, they
were resting, waitin' for me. "Where's this taking us?"
Dorian complained. "We're getting nowhere very fast!"

"Talk soft," I said. "Voices carry. They've passed by
where we turned off, but they'll realize something's
wrong and they'll come a-lookin'."

We had a chance to gain time, so I led off along the
trail. This was wild country, and strange to them, and
Dorian didn't like it much, me leading off thataway. He
wanted to go places that he knew, and that meant to
towns or settlements.

This was lonesome country; until a few years back,
Injun hunting country. We were on the Kentucky side
now, but most of those West Virginia mountains had
belonged to nobody. Here and there Indians lived in
the low country but stayed out of the mountains except
when in pursuit of game.

It was wild country, rough, cut by many small streams, heavily timbered, country but it was my kind of country, the kind where I'd grown up. Settlements were all right for most folks, but a body was too easily seen and followed where other folks abide.

There were folks along the river, however, and once in a while a place hidden back in the hollow. It came to me suddenly that somewhere ahead was the little town of Louisa and that while I'd been thinking poor, I needn't do so longer. We could go into that town and I could buy me a new rifle-gun, biding the time I could recover my own. At least I wouldn't feel so plumb undressed as I did now.

That meant takin' a chance on being caught up with, but having a rifle-gun meant all the difference.

"Mr. Chantry," I advised, "there's a town yonder on the river. I think we'll amble thataway. You better keep your shootin' hand ready, because we'll almost surely run into Felix Horst and some of his outfit."

"At least we can buy a decent meal!" he said. "I am not worried about Horst."

"That's where you an' me differ," I said. "I worry considerable about him. All he's got to do is kill us an' he can take my money and be off with it."

"I don't kill very easy," he commented.

"I hope you don't," I agreed. "You're a right handsome young man and there's not too many about, but that there Horst, he isn't going to come up an' give you a break. He doesn't want to die and he knows he can, so he'll be no damn fool. He'll shoot you from the brush and take what he wants off your body."

We came into the town with the sun hanging low in the sky, and I went first to a store to buy my gun. I'd taken coin from the carpetbag, and sure enough I found what I wanted. I bought me a brand-new rifle-gun like those made in Pennsylvania. Nor did I waste time charging it.

There was a tavern there, and we went to it and put

our feet under their table for supper. "We'll stay here through the night," Dorian said.

Well, I looked at Archie and he shrugged his big shoulders. Both of us knew we'd better light out of there because this was right where Horst and them would come. I will say that meal tasted good and it would give us a chance to wash up.

There was a room with a bed for me, but they'd sleep in the outer room on the floor, wrapped in whatever they wore.

There was one window to my room and the one door that opened into the main room of the tavern. The window was shuttered and locked from the inside. I taken my bag inside and put it down with the rifle-gun and peeked out through the shutter slats. Not far away was the river and a great big old stone house somebody said had just been completed.

The tavernkeeper fetched me a wooden tub filled with hot water, and when I'd bathed and cleaned my clothes some, I felt a whole lot better. I was even beginning to feel Dorian might be right, and then I heard a voice in the taproom and it was Timothy Oats. He was having a drink. Through a crack where the door didn't fit that well, I could see him. He was settin' with Elmer and a big swarthy man, and Dorian was across the room with Archie, a glass of beer on the table in front of him.

Well, I got dressed. By now they would know I was here, and they would have some kind of a plan worked out. Nothing to happen right here in town, maybe, but after we'd gotten out on the road.

This was where the Big Sandy River started, I guess you'd say, the Tug Fork and Levisa Fork joining here to make the Big Sandy. Sometimes, although I'd not have said it aloud, I almost wished I was alone and didn't have those men to worry about. Archie, he was a swamp boy, a swamp and timber boy, and I could see it. If you wanted to call him a boy, that is. He wasn't much older than Dorian but he'd grown up scratchin' for a livin' back in some swamp. I could see it.

He was a trouble-wary man. Part of that came from being black them days. A black man had to ease himself around the tight spots and learned how to keep himself from trouble. Dorian Chantry never had to worry about trouble. Everybody in his part of the country knew who he was and had respect. The trouble was, this wasn't his country.

Sleep was what I was wishful for, but I couldn't lay my head in comfort with him out there in the same room with Tim Oats. Peekin' through the slats, I could see Archie was worried, too. He knew as I knew that Tim Oats probably felt if they could be rid of Chantry they could handle me.

The keeper of the tavern was no fool. When you run a place like that, you learn to sense trouble coming before it happens, and I caught him throwing a glance, one to the other.

If he was worried, he wasn't the only one. What Tim Oats had in mind, I don't know, but something was cookin' and he had the mixture in mind. Tim Oats was between Dorian and the door, and so was that big swarthy man, to say nothing of Elmer.

Dorian finished his beer and stood up. Archie had finished his beer too, but he was still holding the mug. Dorian glanced over at the host. "Do we sleep here? On the floor?"

"It will be warmer, with the fire going." The tavern-keeper wanted no trouble. "You can bed down right here."

Tim Oats exchanged a quick look with the big man, and I guessed this hadn't been a part of whatever they had in mind. Maybe they expected Chantry and Archie to go past them out the door.

Archie moved their table over closer to Oats and his group, putting it between them. He carefully moved the benches, too, kind of walling themselves away from

Oats. It was done naturally, like he was just clearing a
place to lie down, but I must say it was going to make it
hard for that outfit to start anything in the night without
making some noise.

Dorian drew his pistol and checked the loading, then
stretched out on the floor near the fire.

Oats glared at the pistol. "What's that for?" he
demanded.

Dorian smiled that lovely smile of his. "Indians!" he
said. "Wild Indians! Lots of them in these woods! Or
haven't you heard?"

"They been cleared out," Oats protested uneasily.

"Don't you believe it. They come around during the
night, looking for scalps. A man can't be too careful."
He hesitated and his face was innocent as a girl's.
"Now, don't you boys move around too much. If that
door opens in the night or somebody creeps around,
I'm liable to go to shooting."

"Ain't been any Indians around here in years!" the
swarthy man argued.

"Well," Dorian said cheerfully, "if they come, you
are closer to the door than we are, so please stop
them."

Looked to me like everything was going to be all
right, so I went to bed, and tired as I was from the long
night and day of walking, I slept until day was breaking.

When I came out for breakfast in the morning, they
were all at a table. Two tables.

"Ah? Miss Sackett! You do look as if you slept well!
Won't you sit down?" Dorian was smiling and cheerful,
but Oats looked sour. He shot me a quick glance but I
ignored him, making as if I'd never seen him before.
Elmer looked mean, but I would expect that. He was a
young man who needed his sleep.

"Buckwheat cakes and honey!" Dorian said. "This is
living!"

He glanced over at Oats. "Are you gentlemen going
far? I mean, if there is any way we can help . . . ?"

"We don't need no help," Oats said. "Tend to your own affairs!"

"Oh, but we intend to!" Dorian was almighty cheerful, and a body would almost think he welcomed trouble. "It will be no problem."

The buckwheat cakes were good. The coffee was fresh ground like it should be. Once the food was on the table, nobody was inclined to talk, and I was giving thought to what lay ahead. Somewhere to the south was Pikeville, and it would surely be easier if we could find a boat. A canoe would be best, or even a skiff.

When the rest of them had gone outside, I went to the tavernkeeper. "What's going on?" he asked. "I thought there would be trouble."

"They are thieves," I said, "and we're wishful of getting away from them. Is there anybody with a skiff or a canoe?"

"There's an old birchbark canoe. . . ." He pointed. "Yonder, back of the barn there's an inlet. The canoe lies there."

When I started to reach for money, he put up a hand. "No, don't worry about money. I heard them call you Sackett, was that right?"

"It is. I am Echo Sackett, from Tuckalucky Cove, or thereabouts."

"Before we started the inn," he said, "there was a time down on the Big Sandy when I was laid up. I was almighty sick, with a wife and two young-uns. There was a man came through, found us hard up for meat, and he stayed around for a week, huntin' for us, cookin' until we got well, and carin' for us generally. Then he taken off and I haven't seen hide nor hair since. He was a Sackett. So you just take that canoe and do what you've a mind to."

"Bread on the waters," I said, "and thank you."

Outside, Dorian was squatting on his heels, looking off down the street. Timothy Oats was down there with Elmer, talking to another man.

"Come on," I said. "We've got a canoe."

We moved fast, slipping away and into that canoe. A stroke or two of a paddle and we were out of that inlet and turning upstream against the current. I was a fair hand with a paddle myself but I had to admit it, Dorian was better. Of course, he was bigger and stronger. Archie took to a paddle like he was born to it.

How long it took them to discover what happened to us, I wouldn't try guessin', but I've an idea we were long gone before they figured it out. We taken off up the Levisa Fork and we made good time, but I was worried.

We weren't getting away that easy. They would be after us, and they could ride the river too.

They would be coming and we'd be getting into wilder and wilder country. There were scattered towns along the Levisa Fork, but there were long, lonely stretches in between and had an idea they'd gone about as far as they wished.

What worried me even more was Felix Horst. Where was he? So far he'd kept from sight, but I was sure he was around, but bidin' his time.

Timothy Oats or Elmer might just take our money and run, but not Horst. He would leave us dead.

He was that kind of man, and I didn't want to die, nor see Dorian Chantry laid out for burial. The thought gave me a twinge, and he saw it.

"Somebody step on your grave?" he asked.

"Not mine," I said.

Well, he just looked at me, and when I looked over my shoulder at him again, he was dipping his paddle deep, his face serious.

When this was over, all over, I hoped there'd be time to talk, to just set by the river and talk, boy-girl talk. I blushed. Who was I to think such thoughts?

# 16

The river was up but the current was slow and easy-like. We had us a start on those who followed, and we'd best take advantage of it. There was one thing workin' for us they wouldn't know. The further we went, the closer we got to Sackett country.

Dorian had laid aside his coat and was workin' in shirtsleeves. I will say for a city boy he had muscles a body wouldn't expect. Before the morning was over I spelled him on the paddle and got a glimpse of his hands. He hadn't said a word, but blisters were beginning to show. I suspect it had been a while since he'd been that long on a paddle.

The Levisa Fork curved around some, so we couldn't see very far, but I had an idea they were comin' up behind us.

The banks were forested right down to the water in most places, although here and there was a farm and sometimes cattle were down along the river. It was late afternoon before we turned into a little cove and went ashore to make coffee. I found some Jamestown weed and took some leaves from it.

"Put this on your hands," I said. "It will help."

"Thanks," he said, and glanced at the leaves curiously, then at me. But he used them, holding them in his hands.

We ate some bread and slices of meat brought from the tavern. "This will be a killin' fight if they catch up," I warned. "Horst an' them won't be for travelin' any further. They figure they're in wild country now and whatever happens won't be brought home to them."

Dorian said never a word, but I had an idea he was beginning to realize the seriousness of it. Archie, who had been up the creek and over the mountain a few times, he had no illusions.

"How far to the next town?" Dorian asked.

"Few miles. A place called Paintsville. We've been makin' pretty good time," I added, "maybe three miles to the hour or a mite less."

We'd be goin' slower from now on, I suspected, with Dorian's hands blistered the way they were. My hands were used to hard work and I'd spent a sight of time in a canoe on the Holston, the French Broad, and the Tennessee at one time or another. My brother Ethan was a great one for the water, and he'd taken me along many a time when huntin' or fishin'. He had a taste for catfish. I said as much.

"They're in here," Archie said. "Given time, I could catch us a bait. You fix 'em proper an' there's nothin' better. Unless its yellow-jacket soup."

"What?" Dorian looked around at him. "Did you say yellow-jacket *soup*?"

"It's a Cherokee dish. "Et it many a time when I was a boy." He glanced at me. "You must've had it too?"

"A time or two. We were friends to the Cherokee since the first Sackett moved into the far blue mountains. Half the youngsters I knew when I was knee-high were Cherokees. Although all the folks didn't find them so friendly. It was Cherokee and Shawnee who did for the Wiley family. Ever'body," I added, "knew the story of Jenny Wiley."

"Who was she?" Dorian asked.

"Injuns attacked their station whilst all the menfolks were off huntin'. They killed Jenny's brother, and three of the youngsters were killed and scalped. They taken Jenny an' her baby prisoner, finally killed the baby by bashing its head against a tree because it cried too much. Jenny got away finally, and barely made it to safety, with Injuns right after her." I gestured at the country around. "It happened right up the creek from here near a place they called Harmon's Station. It's been gone a long time now."

We paddled on, nobody talking much, and the shadows darkened the ground under the trees, and the tree trunks lost their shapes in the darkness.

Ahead of us a light showed, then another, and we saw a house and a man walkin' from the barn carryin' a lantern. He went to the house and a door opened and he went in and the moment of light was gone. He would be settin' down to supper now, with no worries of trouble behind him, like us.

"All around here and back the way we've come was Lew Wetzel country. Jessie Hughes, he was mostly further east over in West Virginia. They were Injun fighters. Had folks killed by Injuns, and they declared a vendetta against them. Never let up. Wetzel, they say, let his hair grow long a-purpose to tantalize the Injuns with his scalp.

"They wanted his hair but they were scared of him, too. Some of them didn't believe him human."

I taken up a paddle against to spell Archie. "Village ahead." He spoke softly. "We'd better get some grub."

A man was down by the river, watering a team. He looked up as we nosed in to the bank. "You be travelin' late," he commented.

"We're riding ahead of trouble," I said, "and wishful of avoidin' it."

"Ma could put somethin' on." He pointed toward the nearest light. "I'm behindhand with cultivatin'," he explained. "I was laid up with a fever.

"You go on up to the house. Ma will enjoy the comp'ny. She's a great one for comp'ny." He turned his team away from the water. "I can do without, m'self."

A dog ran out, barking fiercely. "Shep," the man said, "you be still. These are folks."

A woman came to the door, a ladle-spoon in hand. "Who is it, Jacob?"

"Strangers, Ma, right hungry ones. I said we'd put somethin' on."

There was a basin on a bench by the door, and a roller towel. We washed up there, and Archie went down by the river again to listen into the night.

"They followin' close?" Jacob asked.

"We don't know, but they'll be along." Archie looked at him. "You be careful. They ain't kindly folks."

"We never turned anybody away," Jacob said.

"I'm not suggestin' it, just you be careful. These are mean folk."

Jacob looked over at me.

"You know the Natchez Trace?" I asked. Of course he did, we all did. "One of these men worked the trace like the Harpes an' Murrell. Only nobody ever caught him at it. The one time they did catch him over in the Settlements, he hired a good lawyer an' went free."

"All right. You have you somethin'." He turned to his wife. "Ma? Fix them a bait of that hog meat. The roasted meat, somethin' they can carry off with them."

He went to the barn with his horses and stripped the harness from them. I was standing tired in the night, and I knew the others were, too. When he set up to the table I could see weariness in their faces. If only we could lay up and rest!

I thought for a minute of takin' that new rifle-gun and

layin' up on a bend of the creek with it. I could fix a
man dead at two hundred yards with that. Maybe five
hundred. But I was not wishful of killin'. Yet I remembered what Regal had said: "There's times when a body
must defend himself, Echo, an' when that time comes,
you'd better win."

There was a fire going on the hearth, and the table
had been spread with a cloth, honorin' the company.
"Ain't often we get folks from the river," the woman
said. "They don't travel the waters the way they did
when I was a girl.

"They're beginning to cut timber up yonder. Logs
will be floated down to the Ohio soon."

"It's cash money," I said, "but I hate to see the trees
go down."

"We need the money," the woman agreed. "Jacob
may take to cuttin' an' fallin' hisself. Not many cash
crops in this here country lest a man goes to moonshinin',
an' we don't hold with that. Not that we're teetotalers.
Jacob likes his nip, time to time."

When we'd eaten, we got up and Archie wiped his
hands on his pants. "Thank you, ma'am. I am obliged."

"Don't forget the bait I put up for you. Take it along
in case of need."

"We will need it," I said, "but take our warning.
Those behind us ride with the devil. They are not
kindly folk."

"We never turned anybody away," Jacob repeated.

"Don't turn 'em away, but keep a gun handy."

We went back to the canoe, hesitated, then got in
and shoved off upon the dark, dark water. All of us
ached with weariness.

"Up ahead," I said, "we'll find a place. We've got to
sleep."

Maybe it was because we were tired. Maybe it was
the idea that men followed us to steal what we had, but
I had a sense of foreboding, a sense of evil.

Where was Felix Horst? It wasn't like him to disappear and leave the stealing to such as Timothy Oats and Elmer. That man worried me.

"Don't worry about him," Dorian said. "He's away behind us, probably in Cincinnati or some such place."

We paddled more slowly now, moving carefully on the dark water because there were occasional floating logs and sometimes masses of debris and drift stuff all rafted together. By day a body could see them easy enough; by night it was another thing. Even a projecting root or branch could rip the bottom out of a canoe like ours.

"Hey!" Archie was peering into the night. "There's a landing of some sort."

"Let's see what's there," I said.

Archie guided the canoe in alongside the dock, and as we steadied the boat, he climbed out.

"Cabin up yonder," he said, "all quiet. I think it's deserted."

We tied the canoe and climbed out, bringing our gear. Somewhere back in the darkness an owl hooted a question to the night.

"Pull the canoe under the landing," I suggested. "If somebody comes along, they aren't apt to see it."

There were big trees here, tulip, sycamore, oak, and suchlike. There was a smell of decay and a sense of emptiness about the place. There were no cows in the lot, no smell of hogs or horses.

"Deserted," Dorian said. "I wonder why."

"They couldn't cut the mustard," I said. "Many try, only a few make it. Some find the work too hard, some can't stand the loneliness."

"Let's see what's in the house," Dorian suggested.

"Leave it be," I said. "If anybody comes a-lookin', that's where they'll go. We can sleep under the trees yonder, and if anybody comes, we'll hear them."

Archie had taken a stick he found leaning against a tree and was brushing around. "Snakes," he explained.

When we sat down and listened, here and there

things rustled in the far-off leaves, branches rubbed one against the other, and now that we were quiet, the frogs started to talk it up again. Occasionally we saw a bat dip and swoop, chasing bugs.

Stretching out on the ground with my arm for a pillow, I stared into the night, wondering where Regal was and if the family worried about me.

It was very dark but our eyes became accustomed to it and we could make out the dim outlines of the cabin, a shed, and a corral. Somewhere we could hear water running, from a spring or a branch, no doubt.

My eyes opened suddenly. I had slept, I do not know for how long. I could hear the breathing of Dorian Chantry, and somewhat father away, that of Archie. The night was still. Yet, what had awakened me?

Something, some sound, some. . . .

I listened, and seemed to hear something moving near me; there was a faint smell. Then the movement sound ceased, but the smell remained.

What was it? It smelled, faintly, like something wet and slimy. A crocodile? Or alligator? I doubted if there would be one this far north, but a body never knew, and they had been found in swamps and bayous off the Mississippi, but the smell was unlike what I would expect from them.

A wet smell, like a wet dog.

That was it! It was the smell of a wet dog, yet what would a dog be doing here, alone? Or was it alone? A dog was rarely a soliatry creature; dogs liked people, were happiest when with people.

My new rifle-gun lay beside me, my pistol was close to hand, the other Doune pistol was still in the carpetbag, also close by.

Something stirred among the leaves and I drew my pistol. I did not want to shoot, for a shot in the night can be heard a far piece, yet. . . .

A few stars were out. I could make out the shadows of things, and through the leaves I could see the silver gleam of the river. I listened, straining my ears. All was quiet.

I wanted to be at home. I wanted to be in my own bed, getting up in the morning to familiar chores. I wanted to sit and talk with ma, I wanted to sew, to darn socks, I wanted to be *home*!

I was tired of running, tired of being hunted, tired of being forever watchful. I wanted to sit with a cup of coffee beside me and watch the shadows lift from the hills of home.

Regal seemed far away now, and Finian Chantry was in another world. I wanted to be home, among decent folks, I wanted to stand beside Ma in church of a Sunday and sing one of the old hymns or maybe set by the fireside of a night and sing "Greensleeves," "Lord Lovell," "Black Jack Davy," or "Rickett's Hornpipe."

Something moved again, and I could just make him out. It was a dog, and he was lying near us, seeming to want company.

"It's all right, boy," I whispered. "Go to sleep now."

And I did.

# 17

He was a shepherd dog, mostly black and brown but with some white on his chest and legs, and he looked like he'd been seeing hard times.

"Where'd he come from?" Dorian wanted to know.

"Joined us in the night. Looks like he's been missing some meals."

Archie was putting together a fire. "Coffee in a bit," he said, "and we can broil some meat."

The landing where we'd left the canoe was made of home-cut planks and was old, all gray and silvery and no place for a body to walk with bare feet. There was moss growing on the pilings and every sign it had been there for a long time.

What happened here? I wondered. It was a good place to live, with water and fine timber. Some fields had been cleared but lying unused for a long time now.

We fed the dog some scraps and when we climbed into the canoe he whined, wanting to come. Dorian looked over at me. "What do you think?"

"Why not?" I said, and Archie spoke to the dog and he hopped into the canoe like he'd ridden in one all his life.

"We may be stealing somebody's dog," Dorian said.

"He's homeless," Archie replied. "I can see it in him. Whoever his folks were, they're gone."

Dorian and Archie did most of the paddling but I'd spell first one, then t'other from time to time, giving them some rest. Once in a while there'd be a long straight stretch and we'd look back and see nothing. Nevertheless, I was worried.

"I'd like to ride this river down, sometime," Archie said, "get back some of the work I've put in goin' upriver."

"There's easier ways to go back," I said, thinking of the steamboats that sometimes came up the river from the Ohio to Nashville.

"I can't wait to get back," Dorian said, and I just looked at him, not wishing for him to go at all.

"Have you a girl back there?" I tried to keep my voice casual.

"A few," he said. "It's a wide field and I play the field."

Well, I told myself, that's better than if there was a particular one.

"We'll have you home soon," he added. "Right back with your folks where you belong. Then I'm catching the first stage, steamer, or whatever back to Philadelphia."

Archie glanced at me but he said nothing, nor did I. Maybe Dorian would be better off in Philadelphia. He did not look as handsome as when he started. His clothes were shabby now, and he hadn't shaved in several days. He always combed his hair real careful and he took time to clean up from time to time.

"Even with the water runnin' high," I said, "we're not goin' much further with this canoe. This turns into just water runnin' over rocks a mite further along."

It was that shep dog who saved us. We'd swung wide to come around some drift-logs and brush gathered at a bend of the creek when that dog suddenly come to his feet, every hair bristling, and he began to bark.

"Backwater!" I yelled, most unladylike, and my voice was drowned in the crashing thunder of rifles firing. I dug in with my paddle and Archie with his. A bullet shattered the paddle in my hands, another ripped the front of the canoe, then the current had us back behind that point of drift-logs, the current and Archie's quick reaction to my yell. There was another shot and then I heard swearing and somebody yelled, ". . . too soon, damn you!"

"Across the creek!" Archie spoke low but quick. "Into the trees!"

The river wasn't wide here and the current helped. For a moment we were visible from upstream and somebody shot, but the bullet missed and then we were back of a timbered point.

We beached the canoe and piled out. "Leave it!" I said.

"Are you hurt?" Dorian was staring at my wrist, which had been cut by flying splinters when the paddle was shot from my hands.

"A scratch," I said. "Let's get away from here!"

They had been laying for us, all set to mow us down, and that shep dog had saved our bacon. When he jumped up and went to barking, he evidently caused those hiding men to shoot too quick. If we'd been a canoe length further up the creek, they'd have killed us all.

We dragged the canoe ashore, taken up our goods and went into the forest.

We had been days on the water and had paid little mind to the forest we were passing through, but this was big timber, giant sycamores, blue beech, river birch, and clumps of black willow, with here and there a table of rhododendrons. There was a game trail taken

off toward the mountains, and we taken it, with me
leading.

Maybe it was forward of me, bein' a girl and all, but
whilst Archie had a knowin' way about him, I didn't
think Dorian when it came to trails would know come
hither from go yonder, so totin' my bag and my rifle, I
just headed off into the tall timber.

What I wanted was a place to hole up and make a
stand. Whoever fired on us would be wanting to finish
us off, and I didn't know how my outfit would do in an
Injun fight amongst the trees. Back toward Pine Mountain there were rock formations, caves, and such. What
I wanted was high ground with some rocks and timber,
a place with a good field of fire.

I'd never been in a shootin' fight but once, when I
was ten, when some raidin' Injuns had come through,
but I'd heard Pa, Ethan, Regal, an' them talk about
what was needed.

That trail didn't amount to much, but it was going
our way and it was climbing along some limestone
ridges and through the timber. Nor did the boys argue
with me. They seemed to want to get shut of those folks
back there just as bad as I did.

Who was it? How had they gotten ahead of us? Or
was this Felix Horst with some of his old Natchez Trace
outlaw friends?

"You'd better let me carry your carpetbag," Dorian
suggested. "Or your rifle."

"Take the bag," I said. "Nobody carries my weapon
but me."

Once, stopping to catch our breath after a climb
through rocks and trees, I said, "We'd better do some
thinkin'. They know where we're a-goin'. They'll cut
across an' get ahead of us again. Somewhere up yonder
they'll be waitin' for us."

"We lucked out this time," Archie said. "That won't
happen again."

We rested there among the pines, watching the coun-

try below us. We were tired, and we were scared. I
know I was, and Archie's face had a haunted look.
Dorian, he was white under the flush the sun had been
colorin' him with. Bein' hunted by men who want you
dead is no way to live. If it hadn't been for that shep
dog we'd all be dead. Where did he come from, out of
the night like that? Whose dog was he? Looked to me
like he'd been on his own a good while, and it might be
his home was far from here.

"We've got to cut them down," I said, "make 'em
understand there's a price to pay."

"You mean kill them?" Dorian was shocked.

"They're tryin' to kill us," I said.

"Your Uncle Finian sure wouldn't hesitate," Archie
said. "That old man's a holy terror!"

Dorian looked around at him. "What do you mean?
Uncle *Finian?*"

"He went down to the Dutchman's," Archie explained,
then repeated the story of the fight in the street.

"Uncle Finian did that?"

"I was with him."

"I can't believe it! Uncle Finian!"

"I can believe it," I said. "That's a tough old gentleman.
I could see it in him."

We moved on, Shep trotting ahead, and believe me,
I felt better with that dog along. Why he adopted us,
I'd never guess, but he surely had.

From time to time we saw deer, and we crossed the
trail of a coon. It was coming on to night before we
found a ledge masked by trees. It was above the trail
we'd been following, and with a fine view of the way
we'd come.

"It's a good place to sleep," Dorian said.

We were wearied by the long day, and nobody was of
a mind to talk very much. There wasn't much left to
eat, but we ate it cold, sharing a mite with the dog. We
were on a ledge, a sort of notch in the rock wall, and it
was a good tight spot.

"Somewhere yonder," I told them, "is a big ol' pine tree, stands by itself. They call that way the Trail of the Lonesome Pine."

They looked where I pointed, but neither had any comment. It was wild, lonesome country with the breaks of the Big Sandy lyin' close by. Right at that moment I wanted most of all just to be home.

We made us a fire you could put in a teacup, almost, and made coffee. When we'd had our coffee, we left the pot on the coals. "You all sleep," I said. "I'll keep watch."

"You?" Dorian said. "Of course not. You sleep. Archie and I will share it."

"There's three of us here," I insisted. "We'll take turn about. That dog's tired too. We shouldn't trust to him."

They slept first, and the wind came down through the pines, moaning a lonesome song. I went over to the little branch that flowed down from a crack in the limestone and had a drink; then I went back to a place I could set with my back against the rock wall and my rifle-gun on my knees.

A couple of times I almost dozed; then I tried making memories come back, something to keep my mind busy. I tried wondering what Regal was doing and how far it was to the Clinch Mountains, where some of us Sacketts lived.

They couldn't be far away. That is, as the crow flies. The trouble was, they had no idea they had kinfolk in trouble. I wished they did. I was scared for me and I was scared for those boys sleepin' yonder. If anything happened to them, I'd never forgive myself.

Right then I began to think like Pa would, or Regal; I began to think about takin' my rifle-gun and playin' Injun down through the woods until I found their camp. If I could catch sight of them, I knew I could leave them with somethin' to bury. A few days ago I'd not have thought seriously of that, but when folks you care about are in danger, you do get to thinkin' such thoughts.

This was a part of the country I knew only from hear-tell, but often of an evening when the boys were settin' around they'd talk of lands where they'd hunted and how the land lay. That's all we knew of much of the country around, yet it was all we needed.

Suddenly that shep dog lifted his head from his paws, he lifted his head and he started to growl, away down deep in his chest.

"Easy, boy!" I whispered. "Easy, now!"

I reached out with my rifle muzzle and prodded Dorian, hoping he'd wake up quiet. There's some who grunt and groan or wake up exclaimin'. He didn't, I'll give him that. His eyes opened and he followed the rifle barrel to me. I put my finger to my lips and indicated the dog, his hackles all bristled up. Dorian reached out a hand, and Archie sat up, drawing his pistol.

The little fire we'd had had gone out, long since. There was no light but from the stars, and few of them. We sat quiet, listening.

We heard faint sounds from the woods, expected sounds. Then a whisper of movement down below where we lay on the ledge. If we kept silent, they might not even guess there was a ledge or a place for us to hide.

I held my rifle-gun ready, but I didn't cock it. That sound could he heard sharp and clear in the night.

A low wind stirred the leaves and moaned through the pines.

My mouth was dry, and I could feel my heart beating, slow and heavy.

Something was moving down there, working its way through the woods. We waited, holding our breath, but it moved off, and after a time we began to breath easy again.

Setting there, to keep myself busy, I rigged a sling with which to carry my carpetbag easier. Something I could hang down my back from a shoulder.

Right back of where I sat was the limestone cliff,
topped with pines and a scattering of other trees. On
my left the cliff broke off and thick forest swept away
down along the mountain.

I stood up, slinging my carpetbag to try it, taking up
my rifle. The dog was not a dozen feet away, peering
into the darkness.

"No, Shep," I whispered. "Ssh!"

I was standing in the shadows and I moved toward
that place where the cliff broke off into the forest. It
was darker there and I would be able to see better
when I looked back.

Dorian was on his feet; Archie squatted against the
rock wall.

Shep came suddenly to his feet, staring at the trees
on the other side of the clearing and growling, low and
deep.

Archie had his gun out, waiting.

"Don't you make a move!" The voice spoke from the
darkness across the way. "Don't you make a move!"

# 18

Three years back, when he saw that wall of water comin' down the gorge, he thought he was a goner. Thing that saved him was that yellow poplar right there on the rising edge of the gorge, and he taken to it, making a fast jump to the first limb and then climbing higher. The water kept him there all day and part of the night, but he'd not forgotten what he saw.

Big old logs were coming down that gorge like shot from a gun, and later when the water was down he went below where they hit the main river, and there they were, all floating pretty as you please in a little bay.

Trulove Sackett was not a man to overlook a thing like that, so he fetched his calk boots and pike pole and he worked out on those logs, cutting the limbs with his ax and bunching them. When he had a log raft made, he packed some grub and floated them down the river to sell.

When fall came and the leaves were dropping from

the trees, he went back up that gorge again, carrying
his rifle-gun. Sure enough, it was as he'd remembered,
a long slope above that gorge, both sides thick with a
fine stand of yellow poplar, with here and there an oak
or, lower down, a sycamore.

That first raft of logs had been happenstance. A body
couldn't depend on such things to make a living by, so
he fetched his cross-cut saw and double-bit ax and went
to work. The cliff was so steep that once he cut a tree it
couldn't do anything but fall, sometimes in the creek
but more often on the side of the creek.

Trulove wasn't worried. Every third or fourth year
there would be a high-water flood on that creek and he
would cut trees and wait.

When the chores were done and there was a fresh-
killed deer hangin' out on the porch for eatin'-meat,
Trulove would fetch his tools to the gorge. It was a long
walk, a good ten miles from home, but he'd carry a bait
with him and a jug of persimmon beer.

First he'd set out on a rocky place he knew, and
restin' that jug on the fork of his elbow, he'd have a
drink, cork her up again, wipe the back of his hand
across his mouth, and give study to that slope, pickin'
each tree real careful so it could get a clear fall to the
creekbed.

If a tree got hung up on that slope, he'd have to get
down there and cut it free, and when a tree that size,
maybe six to ten feet through, when a tree like that
starts to move, a body had better be somewhere else,
fast. So he chose the trees with care to keep the slope
cleared and give them a free fall.

Trulove Sackett was six-feet-six inches tall and weighed
two hundred and fifty pounds and had never found
anything he could take hold of that he couldn't lift.

The folks down to the forks of the creek said Trulove
could jump higher and farther than any man alive, and
run faster, although there was nothing and nobody who
could make him run. That was what folks said about

Trulove, and he just smiled, drank a little persimmon beer, and went back to hand-loggin', which was what he knew best.

He was settin' on that rock studying his next set-to with them yellow poplars when he heard somebody halloo at him.

He knew the voice. He looked down the gorge to where a man was hoppin' from rock to rock to come up the slope. That would only be Macon. Nobody else knew where he was or knew about the loggin' he was doing on chance of a spring flood some year.

Macon Sackett spent most of his time huntin' ginseng to be shipped off to China. In between times he trapped a little fur.

When Macon reached the rock, Trulove handed him the jug and Macon taken a pull. "Now, that's mighty fine drinkin', but a body has to have a taste for it. I know folks can't abide persimmon beer nor brandy."

"That's most of them. Leaves more for us."

Macon studied the slope, then glanced at Trulove. "That's a killer, Trulove," he commented, "that slope is. One o' them big logs will get you sometime."

"Maybe."

Macon hadn't come this far to talk logging, so Trulove waited, taking another pull at the jug. If he was to get anything done, it was time he started. Took a while to fell the big ones.

Macon stropped his knife blade on his boot sole. Sized it up, stropped some more. "You mind that nubbin of a girl from over by Tuckalucky Cove? Echo, her name was?"

"The one who outshot all the boys over at Caney's Fork?"

"That's the one." Macon tested the edge of the blade on a hair. "She's been down to the Settlements to pick up some money due her. Seems like she's on her way home with a couple of pilgrims an' there's somebody after her."

"They better not catch up."

"Oh, she can shoot, all right! She can prob'ly shoot better than anybody, but there's a passel of them." He paused a moment. "One of them is Felix Horst, from over on the trace."

Trulove put the cork in the jug and smacked it with his palm to settle it solid. "Where they at?"

"Word come from somebody down on the Russell Fork. He figured we should know." Macon paused.

"She'll be headed for the Cove. Where's Mordecai?"

"On his way, I expect. Gent who passed the word to me saw him first."

Trulove cached his tools along with the jug, still more than half-full. He picked up a small cache of food, powder, and shot he kept there.

They crossed Big Moccasin Creek and came through the trees to the old Boone Trail. It was not far from here that Boone's oldest son, James, had been killed by Indians, along with several others. That had been back around '73, if Trulove recalled correctly.

They were running smoothly, easily, with the swinging stride of the long hunter.

"Mordecai will get there before we do," Macon said.

"Aye, he'll have the lead on us."

When they slowed to a walk after an hour's run, Trulove asked, "Two pilgrims seein' her home?"

"A big black man and a Yankee, the way it was said. A big young man."

"Honey draws flies," Trulove commented. "As I recall, she was right shapely an' pert."

It was coming on to day-down, with shadows gathering. The two ran on, taking time only to pause for a drink at a cold branch that trickled down the rocks. They rested for a moment, thinking of what lay ahead, and then they were off again, running easily.

"Should come up to that country come dawn. Then we got to find them."

Macon was a long, lean man, a Clinch Mountain

Sackett, as was Trulove, a man given to long periods in the woods hunting for ginseng, usually alone. Yet he had done well, as there was always a market for what he found, and a market that paid well.

No matter, a Sackett was in trouble and they were coming down from the hills to see her safely home or bury the ones who brought her grief. Old Barnabas, him who founded the clan, he laid that down as law more than two hundred years back, and since that time no Sackett had ever failed to come when there was need.

"What do you think?" Trulove asked.

They had slowed to a walk again, and Macon took his time, considering. "We'd better cut for sign around the head of Wallen Creek. There over to Stone Mountain or the Powell. If they've gotten further, we'll know it."

"We'd best watch for Mordecai."

"He'll find us. Nobody can find Mordecai lest he's wishful of it."

An hour before first light they went off the trail into a thicket and put together a small fire and made coffee. They napped by the fire, drank some more coffee, and they listened. Sound carried a ways in the mountains during the still of morning.

"Mordecai will find 'em. He's almighty sly."

"He still make all his own gunpowder?"

"Surest thing you know. He's got several places, one of them a cave over to Grassy Cove. You recall that place Jubal found on his way west?"

"I didn't know he still went there. Folks have settled down there, I hear."

"More'n forty years now. The way Pa tells it, Jubal almost settled down there himself, he liked it that much."

Macon Sackett sat up. "Mordecai trusts no powder but his own make."

They finished the coffee and put their few things into packs. Carefully Trulove extinguished the fire, then scooped dirt to smother the ashes. A moment or two they studied the dead fire, then moved down to the trail.

"Today, you reckon?" Macon knew the question's answer, but Trulove nodded.

From here on they would walk. They could hear better.

When that voice told us not to move, I was in the shadows and I just faded back, easy-like. When I had a big tree betwixt them and me, I waited, my rifle up.

They came out of the woods then, seven or eight of them, and a rough, rough lot. Felix Horst was there, Tim Oats, and Elmer, but there were others I'd not seen before, except for one. He was the last one to come out and I recalled seeing him down to the Cove one time. His name was Patton Sardust and he had been one of the Natchez Trace thieves. A big man, and mighty mean.

Horst looked from Dorian to Archie. "Where is she?"

"Who?" Dorian said.

"Don't give me lip!" Horst's features sharpened. He was a man of no patience; you could see it in him. That was a notch against him. In the wild country, a body needs patience.

Horst stared at Chantry. "Who are you?"

"Dorian Chantry, sir. Not at your service."

"Chantry? Related to Finian?"

"He is my uncle, sir."

Felix Horst swore; he swore slowly, viciously, and with emphasis. He glanced over at Oats. "How'd he get into this? What's he doing here?"

"I told you," Oats insisted. "I told you he was along. I expect the old man sent him."

Horst glanced at Archie. "Runaway slave, eh? Well, you're worth something, anyway."

"He's a free man," Dorian said. "He has always been free."

Horst smiled. "We'll change that. If he isn't a slave, he should be, and I've got just the place for him. They'll teach him who is free."

"What about him?" Patton Sardust said, indicating Chantry. "We don't need him."

"He's Finian Chantry's nephew," Oats protested. "Anything happens to him, we'd never hear the last of it."

"Him?" Sardust scoffed. "No Finian scares me. I'll cut his throat myself."

"You could try," Dorian said.

What could I do? If I started shooting, they'd probably kill the two of them right off. Yet something was going to blow the lid off, I could see that. Whatever else he might be Dorian surely wasn't scared. Might have been better if he had been. Archie, I noticed, had quietly shoved his pistol back of his belt when they first closed in, and nobody had made a move to disarm them.

Where I stood I had a good field of fire and I was no more than thirty yards back into the trees.

"If they moved," Horst said, "kill the white man. That black is worth money."

Then he gestured. "Hans? You, Harry, an' Joe, you scout around and find that girl. Bring her here to me."

What to do? I could ease off through the brush, I could wait right there so we'd all be together, or. . . . They were coming; one of them headed right at me, although I knew he couldn't see me.

They'd stirred up the fire, put wood on, so the place was lit up. If I moved, that man was going to see me, and if I didn't, maybe. . . .

He came around the tree. "Ah!" he said. "I am the lucky one."

The rifle was close by my side and he was not looking for a woman to be armed. Regal had taught me a thing or two, so when he loomed over me and stepped close,

I just jerked up the muzzle of that rifle and caught him right where his chin backed into his throat. I jerked up with it, and hard.

It caught him right and he gagged, choking, and taking the rifle two-handed, I gave him what dear old Regal taught me, a butt stroke between the eyes.

He went down like a poleaxed steer, falling right at my feet, out cold as a stepmother's embrace; then I just faded back into the brush.

The others were closing in on the spot where I'd been, and suddenly the one called Hans gave a yell. "Horst! For God's sake!"

Horst came into the woods. "What is it? What's wrong?"

"It's *Joe*! Look at him!"

Horst came through the trees, then stopped. He swore again. "Bring him into camp," he said brusquely.

"What hit him?" somebody asked. "Look at his face! And his throat!"

"He's still alive," Oats said matter-of-factly, "but he surely ran into something."

Felix Horst straightened up from the injured man. "Chantry? Who's out there? Who did this?"

Before he could answer, there came a weird, quavering cry, an eerie cry that rose and fell, then rose again. It was like nothing they had ever heard, and nothing I had ever heard, either, but I knew what it was.

"What's *that*?" Elmer gasped.

"A ghost," Dorian said. "You've aroused the ghosts that haunt these mountains. You're in trouble now."

"Shut up!" Oats said viciously, anxiously looking around.

"The ghosts," Dorian said, "Echo told me about them. They don't like strangers."

He had called me Echo. He had used my first name!

# 19

From where I was I could see into their camp. The fire was blazing now and the men were drawing toward it but keeping their guns on Dorian and Archie.

That cry had come from afar off—how far, a body couldn't guess on a night like this and in those mountains. It came again, suddenly, wavering, weird, a distant sound in the night.

"A banshee!" Dorian said. "A warning of death to come."

"Yours, more'n likely," one of the men said.

I'd never heard that sound before, but I'd heard tell of it, although there was only one man left who used it. Long ago some of the Clinch Mountain Sacketts had used that cry to warn enemy Injuns they were about, and some Injuns thought it was a death spirit out there in the forest, haunting them, waiting to steal their souls away. The only one I'd heard of using that cry in my time was Mordecai.

He was a long hunter Sackett, not given to the life of

today but clinging to the wild old life of mountains and hunting. Long hunters was what they called those men who went off into the mountains alone to be gone for months, sometimes even years. Dan'l Boone had been one of them, but there'd been a sight of others. Jubal Sackett was one of the first, he'd gone west a long time back, never seen since, although there'd been rumors, stories, and the like.

"Leave him lay," Horst was saying of Joe. "He's been knocked out but he'll be all right."

"But who knocked him out?"

"Maybe 'what' is a better word," Dorian said.

Horst turned on him. He lifted a hand and slapped him across the face. "I told you to shut up!" he said.

If Dorian had struck back, they'd have killed him. He never moved, he just smiled, and that young man went up some notches in my estimation. Maybe he had something to him.

"I think *she* done it," Elmer said.

"A woman? A slip of a girl? To Joe? You ain't serious."

"You don't know her," Elmer said.

Horst looked at Chantry. "Where's that carpetbag? Where is she?"

Felix Horst was mad, I could see that, but worse than that, he didn't know what to do. I could see that in him, too. His instinct was to kill, but he was afraid Dorian was his only clue.

He turned on Dorian. "That Sackett girl? Is she sweet on you?"

Well! There was an answer I strained my ears to hear. "Her? Of course not. She's never thought of me that way."

Little did he know!

"Travelin' through the woods together?" Sardust scoffed. "Who'd believe that?"

"I would," Archie said. "She's a lady."

Bless him!

Somebody added fuel to the fire and brought out a

coffeepot. Some of this I could see; the rest I could surmise.

They moved suddenly and disarmed both men, then sat them down against a log.

At the foot of a stump, in a hollow under the roots, I cached my carpetbag, leaving the Doune pistol in it. I kept my rifle and the pistol with the sawed-off barrel. I worked around through the trees and listened, watching. If they made a move to harm either of those men, I was going to go to shooting, no matter what it cost me.

"When daylight comes," Horst said, "we will find her tracks. No use to go off half-cocked. She can't move fast in those skirts, and you can bet she's not far away. No matter what they say, I think she's sweet on Chantry here."

"You had better think about him," Elmer said suddenly. "If anything happens to him, old Finian Chantry will never let up. He'll track down every one of us."

"What I want to know," one of the men said, "is what screamed?"

"Panther, more'n likely. I've heard they have a funny cry, like a woman's."

"That didn't sound like no woman I ever heard," Sardust said.

"There was a man roamed this country years back, an' Injun hunter name of Lew Wetzel. He had a cry like that. Like a ghost in the woods, he was, and could run like a wolf."

"That's been years ago," another man protested.

They drank coffee and munched on some hard biscuits and meat. My stomach growled, a most unladylike sound. I sat down where I could watch their camp and kept my rifle where it could be used. There was a little blood on the sight. I wiped it off.

Several of them stretched out to sleep, but not Patton Sardust. "When killin' time comes around," he said to Horst, "I want him." He pointed a middle finger at Dorian.

"Who will help you?" Dorian said. "You couldn't do it alone."

Sardust grinned, showing some broken teeth. "We'll see about that." He drew his knife. "Right across the throat, ear to ear, with this."

The mutter of their voices lowered as several men slept, and I could no longer hear. Felix Horst sat with his back against a tree, staring at Chantry, but he was listening, too, so I did not move.

Dead tired, I sat watching their camp, wondering what I could do to get them free, what I could do to fight back without endangering them, and me so tired I could scarcely lift a hand. With the coming of daylight they'd be fanning out in the woods, and I could not avoid them all. Daylight would be a killing time. I could see it coming.

Suppose that weird cry had been Mordecai? But how could he know about me? Maybe it was a painter, a panther, that is. Or maybe it was Mordecai just a-travelin'? I didn't know those Clinch Mountain Sacketts, although we were surely in their part of the country.

Worst of it was, if anything happened to me, my folks would never get that money, and the Good Lord knew they needed it!

What could I *do*? What *could* I do?

It would be growing light soon and those men would be after me, yet I dared not run away into the woods for fear of what they might do to Dorian and Archie.

Maybe if I just went to shooting, those boys could make a break for it? But what would their chances be of gettin' into the woods without being shot? Mighty slim.

I didn't even know rightly where I was, or whether I was still in the state of Virginia or had crossed into Tennessee. I knew the direction I had to travel if I got away. For that matter, I could dig up my carpetbag and head off down the country and maybe get away, but I'd be leaving them in the lurch and I couldn't do it.

Day was coming and I'd better get set to make my

fight. Maybe I was only a girl, but I was a dead shot
and I could nail one of them and maybe reload before
they got to me. I could get one, and when they rushed
me, I could get another with the pistol, and then they'd
have me. And I had no doubt what would happen then,
me bein' a girl and them the kind of men they were.

I was scared for Dorian and Archie, and I was scared
for me.

Elmer got up and walked to the fire. He taken up the
pot and started to fill his cup. I could see Horst and
Oats and three others, one of them the sick man whom
I'd hurt. Something jumped inside me.

*Where were the others?*

Had I dozed? Had they slipped out of camp? Were
they coming for me now?

Something stirred in the brush and I came up fast
and they were on me, two of them, a long, slim dirty
man with a scraggly beard, and a younger one, grinning
at me. Too late for the rifle. As the long thin one
grabbed at me, my hand went into that slit pocket in
my skirt, and I said, "Who is first?"

He hesitated just for a moment, caught by my words,
and I let him have seven inches of blade right in the
middle of him.

He let out a gasp and his face turned kind of greenish
white and I shoved him free and taken a long, swinging
swipe with my blade at the second one. He jumped
back, then picked up an arm-long branch and swung it
at me. It missed, but he was coming on in when I heard
a yell from camp, then a shot and a crashing in the
timber.

"Get them, dammit! *Kill* them!"

Guns exploded, but that young one was coming at
me with that club.

Then somebody was running up on us and he turned
sharp around to see, and it was Dorian who came in
swinging a fist. The fellow with the club drew back for a
swing, but Dorian, just like he'd fought somebody with

a club before, went right into him, slugging him on the jaw, and then, as the fellow went down, Dorian grabbed me. "Come *on*!" he said, and I grabbed up my rifle and we ran.

We ran into the deeper woods. We heard guns firing, and one bullet knocked bark from a tree close by, spattering us with fragments.

We ran, we fell down, scrambled up, ran some more. In a dense growth of trees, all tall, towering yellow poplar, we pulled up, gasping.

"You all right?" he asked.

"I am. You?"

"I guess," he said. "What happened to Archie?"

He was asking himself more than me, because I wouldn't know. All was suddenly still. Not a sound in the forest. We weren't scot-free by any means, and we knew it. I had my rifle in my hands and somehow he had come up with one, evidently one that had belonged to one of the two men who attacked me.

"That other man?" Dorian whispered. "What happened to him?"

"He must've run into something," I said. "It wasn't quite light yet."

"I've got to go back for Archie," he whispered.

"You stay out. He knows a sight more about woods fighting than you do. Maybe he got away."

He was restless, but he waited. "We saw a chance," he said, "and made a run for it."

"You done right," I said.

They would be coming for us soon. He looked over at me. I was crouched down behind the trunk of a big sycamore partly shielded by a limb that was almost as large as the trunk, all mottled kind of gray and yellow.

Resting my rifle, I studied the brush and the trees, looking for a target. They had not located us yet, but they would. There were large trees all around, most of them yellow poplar.

We'd been shot with luck. Undoubtedly back there

I'd closed my eyes for a moment and those men had slipped out of camp and closed in on me. Then the boys had made their break.

"We've got to shorten the odds," I said. "We've got to cut down a few of them."

"I've never killed a man," he said.

"Neither have I, but these here don't seem to be leaving us much choice." I paused a moment. "That money may not seem like a lot to you, but it is a change of life for we-uns back in the hills. It can make things easier for Ma and can ease things for all of us. I came down from the hills to get what was rightly mine and don't intend for it to be taken from me."

Something moved out there, and my rifle came up, resting on that thick branch. Dorian, he slipped a mite further away to take another stand.

Nothing stirred; then something did. Taken me a minute to realize what I had sighted. It was a knee.

The man was well hidden by a slanting log, but he'd drawn up his knee and exposed it. He was sixty yards off and the light was bad but better than that on many a wild goose I'd killed for meat. I taken a bead and squeezed off my shot. The rifle leaped in my hands and that knee disappeared. Only there was a red splotch of blood on the leaves.

"You hit something?" he whispered.

Me, I was reloading. "I never shoot unless I do," I said. "I don't like to miss."

He just looked at me, and I figured: Echo, you're doin' what Regal warned you against. So I said, "His knee was out there, so I tried. He's one they'll have to carry back."

"I wish I knew what happened to Archie."

"So do I, but I think we'd better fetch ourselves out of here before they surround us." I got up. "Let's go."

We eased out of those trees and found a game trail angling down through the woods. We taken it careful, keeping low and heading as near to south as we could, south and west.

"Only way we can help Archie," I said, "is to stay alive. If he isn't dead already, they will try to keep him alive and sell him. We'll find him then and see he's freed, if I have to bring all the Sacketts down from the hills."

"How many are there? Of the Sacketts, I mean?"

"Nobody rightly knows, but even one Sackett is quite a few."

We walked along the creekbed, which was scarcely ankle-deep, then crossed to the other side and went into a stand of slender trees. After a bit, finding a place where we could remain hidden yet see all that approached us, we sat down to rest.

We had come several miles, and neither of us was up to further travel, and we were hungry.

"You catch some sleep," Dorian said. "I'll watch."

For a moment there my eyes were open, and then they were closed and I slept and dreamed, all sorts of wild dreams. It was dark when he shook me awake.

"It will have to be you," he said. "I can't keep my eyes open longer."

Sitting up, I drew my rifle across my lap. It was dark and we could see nothing but the shadows and the stars.

In the moment his eyes closed, I heard that scream, that same wild cry, rising and falling weirdly.

Dorian opened his eyes. "There it is again!" he whispered. "What can it be?"

"Sleep," I said. "All's well here. You just rest."

I didn't like to even think how hungry I was, but what worried me most was that cry. It was nearer this time, and it sounded like the cry of a hunter—hunting what or who, I did not know.

"You sleep," I said aloud. "I'll keep watch."

Yet my eyes were heavy. It was hard to stay awake.

# 20

Patton Sardust squatted on his heels, rifle in hand, and studied the country below him and to the north. It had been some time since he had hunted this part of the country, but that should be the North Fork of the Clinch down there, and over beyond it, the Sinks.

Felix Horst stood beside him, also staring at the country below. He was hoping for smoke, yet doubted they would be so foolish as to build a fire.

"We been underratin' that girl," Sardust said. "We've got to settle down to trackin', movin' in slow an' easy."

"I don't want that black man killed," Horst said. "He's worth an easy thousand dollars if he's in good health."

"How much is she carryin'?" Sardust asked.

Felix Horst knew, but it was not something he cared to tell. Elmer knew, and so did Timothy Oats. That was already two too many.

"She's carryin'," he said, "enough to make it worthwhile."

161

"I think she's cached it," Elmer said.

Horst looked around irritably. "Now, why would she do that? She's on her way home."

"I caught a glimpse of her yonder in the trees. She didn't seem to be carrying a carpetbag. She had a rifle—"

"What's a woman doin' with a rifle?" Collins asked.

"She's a mountain girl," Sardust replied. "They grow up with rifles. Chances are she can shoot."

"Somebody can," Elmer said. "Baker's knee is busted and he's in bad shape. We've got to get him to a doctor."

"You get him there," Horst replied, his tone sharp. "I want that girl and her money."

"You got three men laid up," Elmer insisted, "and I think she done it all. One man knifed, one with his face bashed in, and Baker's knee shot away. I think—"

Horst turned angrily. "Close your trap! I know you're White's man, but any more talk like that and you get out of here! Do you get that?"

"It ain't going to be easy getting those men out of here," Elmer said, and then he added, "if you intend to."

For a moment there was silence, a cold, dead, heavy silence. Elmer involuntarily took a step back, but Horst ignored him.

"You're the best tracker," he said to Sardust. "Can you find them?"

"As long as she stays with him, we've got a chance. Those boots of his leave tracks, and he's no woodsman. She's easy on her feet and she's light anyway, so she leaves mighty little to see. Also, she's canny where she puts her feet."

Oats had been quiet until now. "Suppose Elmer's right and she's cached the money? Maybe we're chasin' her for nothing."

"I want her," Horst said. "She needs to be taught a lesson."

"Who does that pay off?" Oats objected. "I want the money."

"So do we all," Horst replied. He turned to Elmer. "Where was she when you saw her without the carpetbag?"

"It was just before Baker got shot. I saw her clear, but she was gone before I could get my rifle up. She did not have the carpetbag."

"Then she's cached it," Sardust said. "We can back-track her right to where it is."

Horst did not like it, but he kept his mouth shut. He wanted her and he wanted the money and he wanted it all for himself, yet if she had cached it. . . .

Well, when it came to that, he thought he was as good at reading sign as Sardust. In his years along the Trace, he had learned a lot. He had no intention of sharing what he found with any of them, and that included James White.

"Elmer," Horst said, "those wounded men need care. You stay in camp and do whatever you can. Patch up that knee and put a splint on it. We can get him down to the river and float him down to a town.

"Meanwhile, we'll scout around. They haven't gone far."

Oats avoided Elmer's eyes. Elmer did not like it, but he knew better than to cross Felix Horst. He had already said too much. Yet he did not like it out here in the woods and he did not know a thing about wounds or wounded men. He had an idea all three were worse off than anybody admitted; Elmer also had a good idea that Horst intended to abandon them, and maybe him. He should have kept still about her not having the carpetbag. Then he could have looked for it himself.

"I scouted around some," Sardust said, "and I think I know where they're at. Let's go get 'em."

When they were gone, Elmer added grounds to the coffee on the fire and dug around in his pack for some cold biscuits.

Baker looked over at him. "You goin' to patch up my knee?"

"I'll try. I'm not much good at such things."

"Get a splint on it and some kind of bandage. If you can get me down to the creek, we can float down and I won't have to walk, which I can't do anyway."

Gingerly Elmer went to work. He cut away the pants leg a little more and removed the crude bandage. The sight of the smashed knee made him sick and he started to retch. Baker swore at him. "Shut up, damn you! You only got to look at it, I got to live with it."

With a spare shirt from Baker's small pack he bandaged the wound, then rigged splints to keep it stiff. Baker was suffering considerable pain, but it showed only in his eyes or an occasional catch of the breath.

"You get me out of this, young feller, an' my kinfolk will make it up to you. Just get me down to the river."

He filled a cup for Baker and then went to where Harry lay stretched out. Harry had been stabbed, a thrust from low down, driven sharply up. The knife had just cleared his belt and had gone in under the ribs.

Harry stared at him as Elmer checked the wound. He knew nothing about such things, and although the slit was inflamed, there wasn't much blood this time. There had been quite a bit when they first got to him.

"She was such a little thing," Harry muttered, "I didn't figure. . . ." His voice trailed off into nothing, and he closed his eyes.

Joe lay on his back, both eyes blacked and swollen shut, a great lump where his brows should be and his nose broken. She or somebody had hit him with a rifle butt, and he looked awful. There was nothing Elmer could do, and he went back to the fire and filled his cup.

He had to get out of here. If he stayed, Horst would kill him. Horst didn't care about these men, either. They were thieves or river roughs hired on for the job.

Suppose, just suppose he could find the carpetbag?

Then he could get out of here and leave them all. He could go back to Philadelphia. . . .

Maybe not. White would be after him for explanations. Maybe Pittsburgh, or even New York. New York? With money in his pocket. . . .

He closed his eyes and tried to think of where they had been and how she must have moved. From time to time there had been glimpses of her. She'd still had the bag when she clobbered Joe, so she must have hidden it close by.

Elmer thought it all out, trying to remember how Harry had gone out to catch her and where that fight had taken place. She must have been close by, perhaps within a few hundred yards.

He sipped his coffee and thought it through, trying to remember the various places he had seen out there. In among the trees there wasn't much brush, although there were fallen logs, branches, occasional clumps of some brush he did not recognize. Some places under the trees were bare and could be eliminated. After all, the area was not that large, and he should be able to find it.

He got to his feet. Baker had dropped off to sleep, and only Harry was aware. When he started to move away, Harry said, "You comin' back?"

Elmer pointed. "There's my pack. I'm just scoutin' around."

Harry closed his eyes, and Elmer stepped out beyond their sight. Although he was not aware of it, he had changed a lot in these past two weeks. For the first time in his life he had become aware of his own vulnerability. Injury and death happened to others, not to him, but suddenly he realized it could happen to him. He also realized that Felix Horst had no intention of sharing that money with anybody, and anybody who got in the way would be eliminated. So why not find it for himself and get away scot-free?

He wouldn't mind sharing with Tim Oats, but Tim

was with Horst and would have to make out as best he could.

Elmer had learned from James White. He had learned to think before he acted, and now he carefully eliminated various areas beyond the camp, where he would not have to look. It would have to be somewhere she could have hidden, somewhere not easily seen from camp.

Elmer studied the woods before him. There were many large trees, a number of fallen, rotting tree trunks, a few clumps of brush in the more open areas. At one place a huge old giant of the forest had started to topple, but its branches had caught in the branches of other trees and left the tree hanging, its great root mass partly ripped from the earth.

Elmer moved out, searching the ground for tracks. He had never spent time in the woods or wilds, knew nothing about tracking, yet the tracks of the men who had gone out to capture Echo Sackett were plain enough.

She had stabbed Harry. It would have to be her. Who would ever expect a pretty little thing like that to have a knife? Or that she would use it?

That time he had suggested walking her home. He had thought that maybe, on one of those dark streets. . . .

His brow broke into a cold sweat. Why, she probably had that knife then. It would have been him who got stabbed. The thought gave him a queasy feeling in the stomach. Cold steel had that effect on some people.

Elmer paused, looking all about him; then slowly he began to walk. He counted his steps, stopping every few yards to look all about him. When he had walked two hundred steps, he walked several yards to the east and then turned about on a route parallel with his first and walked slowly back, searching the ground with his eyes as he moved.

This was no time to be careless. He was going to work this out bit by bit. When they came back, if they did come back, he could be just scouting, but he hoped he would find the bag and be long gone by the time they returned.

There was a place where the sunlight splashed a clearing in the woods, and there was a tangle of wild rose there. He looked at it but could see no trail through, nor where any bush had been trampled down or broken. There was a profusion of the wild roses there, all pink and lovely in the sunlight. He stood for a moment, caught by the lonely beauty of the place, then shook it off and walked away, frowning at some transient thought.

What was he doing here, anyway? Why had he come? He had come because White had sent him, but was he to be White's errand boy forever? Or was he to go his own way? With this money he would have a start, he would go away, leave White behind, and perhaps study law for himself.

He paused again among the trunks of the great trees. How still it was! How beautiful a place! He did not recall ever thinking of beauty before. He had been sly, cheating, prepared to do White's bidding, no matter what.

He remembered Echo Sackett's cool reaction to his innuendos, if they could be called that, and for the first time he felt shame. There had been something about her, small as she was, a kind of quiet dignity that left him uneasy. Then Finian Chantry had come and Elmer had felt ashamed for James White. He had thought White was quite a man, important and shrewd. Suddenly he saw White dwarfed and he knew he could never respect him again. Finian Chantry had put him in his place quietly but firmly.

Thinking left Elmer uneasy. He was not used to it, and ethics had never concerned him. Why was he thinking like this? Was it she who had started him? Or Finian Chantry? Or was it something about the silence here? He was uneasy, eager only to be away.

On the fourth march of two hundred steps he drew near the toppled tree, its top caught in the branches.

He looked up at it, held so insecurely. He looked again, and swung his path a little wide of it.

When he started back, he was on the far side of the tree, and it was not until he had passed it that he turned to look back at the great mass of uplifted roots.

"Of course," he muttered. "Why not?" He turned and walked back and stood looking at the shallow pit where the roots had been torn from the ground. It was almost filled with leaves.

He stood for a moment, looking around. He was sure this was the place, yet he was suddenly uneasy.

Suppose somebody saw him? Suppose Felix Horst returned before he could get away?

Get the carpetbag and leave at once, right down the mountain to the river. He did not know what the river was, but there would be towns along the river, a place where he could catch the stage or a steamboat and get back to civilization.

He glanced quickly around. All was still; there was nobody. So why did he feel uneasy?

What was bothering him? He went down into the pit, waded through the leaves, kicking with his feet to find it.

His toe hit something yielding. He brushed away the leaves, and there it was.

The carpetbag! The gold! And all his!

He grasped the handle and straightened up and turned.

Patton Sardust was standing on the rim of the pit, his rifle in his hands.

"Now, ain't that nice?" he said softly. "And just the two of us. Nobody else. Just you an' me."

# 21

Sunlight was falling through the leaves, weaving a web of gold and shadow, when my eyes opened. Dorian's coat was over me, and I sat up suddenly, frightened.

"Did I fall asleep? On watch?"

"You did not," he said. "You awakened me when you knew you couldn't stay awake, then you went to sleep as though you'd never slept before."

"What's happened?"

He shrugged. "Nothing I know of. I've heard some movement out there, but nothing close. We'd better get ready to move." He looked around. "What happened to the dog?"

Getting up, I brushed off the leaves and straightened my clothes, wishing there was somewhere to bathe. I felt grimy and my hair would look a sight.

"I think we'd better get your carpetbag and leave," he said. "We'll get to a settlement of some kind, then I'll get help and come back and look for Archie."

"All right." There was no more run in me. I was tired

and I wanted to be home and take the money to Ma. Rightly it was mine, but in my mind it was ours, and that was the way it was going to be.

Quiet as we could move, we worked our way down through the trees. No way I could forget that great hanging tree where I had left the carpetbag. We were still a good sixty yards off when I saw it, and we stopped, looking carefully around. Their camp had been just beyond. Now there was no smoke, nor smell of smoke, and no sound or movement. Still, we waited.

We were almost to the edge of the pit left by the torn-up roots when I saw the tracks. For the first time I felt panic. If somebody had found that money. . . .

I ran down into the pit, scattered the leaves, wading from side to side.

It was gone!

"They've taken it?"

Dumbly I nodded. I fought to keep the tears back. After all our trouble, after all this, I had failed my family, I had failed Ma, I had failed Regal, I had failed Finian Chantry and his efforts to help. I said as much.

"Maybe not," Dorian said. "Maybe not. Let's go after them. Uncle Finian sent me to see you got home safely with your money, and that's just what I am going to do!"

I nodded, unable to speak. They were gone, and the money was gone.

"I wish I was a better tracker," Dorian said, studying the ground.

It brought me back to reality. "I can track. I've been tracking game since I was knee-high."

Of course, I had seen all their tracks, and once a body has tracked, he or she just naturally registers things in the mind. That was Elmer. He had big flat feet and he toed out when he walked. No question about him.

"And that"—I pointed to another track on the rim of

the pit—"that's the big fellow. Patton Sardust, I heard him called. Looks to me like Elmer was in the pit an' Sardust came up on him. Or they came together."

"What about Horst?"

"No tracks of his here, nor Oat's either." I began to cast about. Those two had walked away together. In some places where there were no leaves I could see the tracks better.

"Elmer's got my carpetbag," I said.

"How can you tell?"

"Walkin' away from the hole back yonder, his right foot makes a deeper track. He's carryin' weight in his right hand."

We walked away, following them. They were not wasting time moving out of the area. "Heading for the river," I said. "They don't plan to share with the others."

"Or with each other, probably," Dorian said cynically.

He was learning. Maybe he knew more all the time than I'd expected. "We'd better be careful," I said. "Horst was looking for us. He has Hans with him, maybe somebody else. There must have been eight of them, including the men Horst rounded up."

We talked no more. The trail was plain enough, but occasionally Elmer and Sardust were pausing to look around. They were scared, too. Watchful, anyway.

We were doing some looking around ourselves. At least Dorian was. I had my eyes on their trail, not to lose them.

"Eight?" Dorian asked. "Are you sure?"

"Some of them are out of it. One of them's got him a busted knee. I'd guess three are out of action."

"Elmer and Sardust are ahead of us. That leaves Horst, Oats, and at least one more if our figuring's right."

"It's pretty close," a voice said, and I looked up to see Timothy Oats standing there with the one they had called Hans. My rifle was on them, but Dorian was standing with his feet spread apart, staring at Oats, who was staring right back.

"You fire that gun," Oats said to me, "an' Felix Horst will be here. He's in a killing mood."

"So am I," I replied.

"Don't be foolish," he said impatiently. "You two haven't a chance. They are all around you. Whatever happens here will be forgotten when we leave here. Nobody will even find your bodies."

"You don't know this country, mister. There's folks coming and going all the time."

"No matter. We will be gone. Give us that carpetbag and we will let you go. At least you will have a running start."

"We haven't got it," Dorian said. "Two of your crowd have it."

"You're lyin'!"

"Where's Elmer?" Dorian said. "And where is that big fellow, Sardust?"

Oats was staring at Dorian. "You've got too much lip."

Dorian smiled. "You're supposed to be some kind of a fighter," he said. "Why don't you see what you can do about it?"

"Dorian!" I said.

"This is something I have to do, Echo," he said. "It won't take long."

Timothy Oats took off his coat and laid it on a stump. He put his rifle across it.

"You," I told Hans, "stay out of it."

"Why not? Tim will make mincemeat of him."

I was afraid of that myself, but the way they were looking at each other, like two prize bulls in a pen, I knew nothing I could say would make any difference. Dorian had shucked his coat, too.

He was a shade lighter than Oats, but just as broad in the shoulder.

"You won't find him so pretty when I get through with him," Oats said.

"You take care of yourself, mister. Pretty is as pretty does."

Oats tried a left, drawing Dorian out, or trying to. Dorian ignored the left, moved to the left. He feinted a left, and when Oats moved to counter, hit him with a solid right that shook Oats to his heels. It surprised him, too. He had not expected that, and I could see his expression change. Now he knew he was in for a fight.

Oats was the wilier, ducking, slipping away from punches, hitting hard in return. Twice he landed hard to the body and I winced for Dorian, but he seemed to pay it no mind.

Then they were at it, hammer and tongs, both of them slugging, toe to toe and neither backing up a bit. Oats was hitting Dorian, but Dorian was taking them standing, and suddenly he feinted a left, and Oats, too eager, stepped in and took a right on the chin. It staggered him, and Dorian followed up, swinging both fists to the body.

Oats backed up, tried to get set, but Dorian gave him no chance. The less experienced of the two, he was younger, in better shape, and just a little quicker.

Oats rushed, tried to butt, and Dorian hit him with an uppercut, and when the head came down again, he grabbed Oats by the hair and jerked him forward, kicking his feet from under him. Oats came down hard, landing on his face.

At that moment Hans lunged forward, and I put a bullet through his ear. The shock and the pain stopped him, and his hand went to his bloody ear. I had the pistol in my hand.

"The next one kills," I said. "Just back off."

"You missed," Hans said.

"I didn't want to kill you. I wanted an ear and I got it. You now have one ear. Do you want to try for none?"

The blood was covering the side of his face and his shoulder. He backed off warily.

Oats was getting up, and Dorian was letting him. Suddenly Oats dived at him, grappling for Dorian's knees. He got one of them, right in the face. He staggered and went to a knee. Maybe that boy could fight after all, I thought. This wasn't party games.

Hans had backed off, trying to stop the bleeding. "I'll kill you for that!" he said.

"You haven't done very well so far," I replied. "You just better look at your hole card. You aren't holding very much."

Dorian was bloody himself. He had a cut on his cheekbone and his lip was puffy, but he seemed happy. He was standing, ready for Oats to get up.

"You're a smarter fighter than I am, Mr. Oats," he said, "but you've had too many beers."

"Dorian? We've got to get out of here. We've got trouble coming."

He picked up his coat and put it on, then got his rifle. Oats had reached his coat and was standing over it, about to pick up the rifle he had laid down.

"Go ahead," I told him, "if you feel lucky."

"Horst will be coming. He will have heard that shot."

Dorian made no reply, nor did I. We backed off, watching them as we left. Oats was wiping his bloody face.

"Have you got their trail?" Dorian asked.

"They will have heard that shot too," I said.

"But they won't know who shot, or why. They may travel a little faster."

Elmer and Patton Sardust. I wondered how long Elmer would last. He was just a big gawky boy, and Sardust was a mean man, a hard man, a man who had been through it. They must be near the river by now.

We did not talk, being wishful to make no sound. The tracks were easy to follow, as nobody was trying not to leave a trail. They were headed down the steep slope toward the river. If we could get that carpetbag back, we could just keep going. The direction was right.

There was no need to track them now, as they were on a trail down to the river. I squinted away toward the river. I did not know rightly where I was, and that might be the Powell or it could be the Clinch. We'd been switching back and forth in the mountains, and all I knew was my general directions.

During a pause to catch our breath, I reloaded my rifle-gun. This was mostly new country for me.

There was a path along the river that had been followed by both men and game, and their tracks were there.

Elmer clutched the carpetbag, switching it from his right to his left hand. He wished they'd never found it. He knew the big man walking with him intended to kill him, he knew Sardust wanted it all. For a moment Elmer was inclined to turn and simply hand it to him, but there was a deep stubbornness in him that refused. Anyway, it might not suffice. Sardust might kill him anyway.

Tree shadows fell along the path. He wished he could be walking here alone, without Sardust. He liked the sound of the river.

He stopped suddenly, and Sardust stopped. "What's the matter?" The big man was irritable but watchful.

"I thought I heard something."

"The wind, maybe. Or the river."

"Something else, somebody moving."

"You're crazy!"

"Patton, we should give this back. To that girl, I mean. We should give this carpetbag to Echo Sackett. It's hers."

"You *are* crazy! There's money in there, boy. Money for both of us. Give it back? Why?"

"It's hers. It will mean a lot to her. I know, I was all for stealin' it myself. I didn't like her one bit, but she's got nerve. And she needs this.

"Ever since I got down in this country, I been wonderin' about all this. I figure we're doin' wrong."

Patton spat into the dust. "Well, of all the weak, mollycoddlin' . . . !"

"I mean it, Mr. Sardust. I don't feel the same no more. Men have been hurt over this. Three men down and hurt, an' everybody is for just leavin' them. I don't feel right about it."

"You just give it to me. I'll take the blame. You can run off an' do what you like. I'll just let you off the hook. Give it to me."

"No, Mr. Sardust, I may be a damn fool but I'm takin' it back to that girl. Maybe it's this country, maybe it's her, maybe it's those men back there, dyin' maybe. I don't feel right about it no more."

"You give it to me. I'll shoulder the blame. You run off an' have a good cry. You an' your conscience." Patton Sardust spat contemptuously. "You're nothin' but a damn mollycoddle!"

"No, Mr. Sardust. I am takin' it back to her."

"Shut up! Just give me that bag!"

"I think he's right, Mr. Sardust." The voice came from the trees near the trail. "I think he's right. I think you better leave him go, Mr. Sardust."

A man stepped into the open trail, a very tall, very lean man with a rifle.

Patton Sardust turned slowly. Whatever Elmer did was of no immediate concern. He had never seen this stranger before, but his every instinct told him he was in trouble, deep, serious trouble.

His heart was pounding slowly, heavily. His rifle was by his side, held in the trail position. His hand was almost in the right place. If he could only get his finger on the trigger. . . .

"Who the devil are you?"

"Not the devil, Mr. Sardust, but like him, I can open the gates to hell. I'm Mordecai Sackett. You ready to go?"

# 22

Elmer walked back up the path toward the clifftop. He walked easier, and he felt better. He stopped at one point and looked down through the trees at the river. He just stood there, light and shadow falling over him, and no sound but the trees. He had never known such quiet, never such peace.

From behind him and below there was a shot, closely followed by another.

So that was the end of that, and it might have been the end of him, too.

He had looked into that stranger's face and he had no doubt about who killed whom.

He was dipping down again now, as the track he was following returned briefly to the river before starting up again. He stopped once more, putting the carpetbag down.

He would not know how to get along in country like this, but he could come back to visit. He could walk this trail again, but with no worries.

She came along the trail toward him and he picked up the bag and held it out to her. "This is yours," he said.

"Thank you, Elmer. You are a nice man."

He blushed. "Well, it's yours. I just thought. . . ."

"Thanks."

Dorian came down the trail behind me. "We heard a shot."

"Yes, sir. It was him, I believe. I think he killed Patton Sardust."

"Killed him? Who did?"

"He came out of the woods like a ghost. He looked like a ghost. He said his name was Mordecai Sackett."

"Mordecai!"

Dorian glanced at her. "Is he related to you?"

"He's a Clinch Mountain Sackett. A cousin, sort of."

"There were two shots. I'll go see if he's been hurt." Dorian hesitated. "You'll be all right."

When he had gone, I just stood there staring after Elmer, who was walking away up the trail. Whatever had come over him?

. What would he do now? Could he go back to working with James White? Or would he want to go back?

Now I could go home. Now I had money again, and what I could do would brighten all their lives. I picked up the carpetbag, and Felix Horst was standing there. His pistol was in his hand and he indicated a dim trail toward the river.

"Walk that way. If you call out and he comes, he'll never know what hit him."

"He's not alone down there."

"Get along! Don't try any tricks on me. Just move!"

"Mordecai Sackett's with him. He killed Patton Sardust."

"Get along. Right down the path. You walk easy, and maybe you'll be alive tomorrow."

I walked along, carrying the bag. I had left my rifle on the ground where they would find it. Horst had

seemed to pay no attention. Maybe if I had tried to pick
it up, he would have shot me. Dorian would be coming
back. He would find it right there at the path down
which Horst was taking me.

It led to the river. There was a clearing there, cut off
from the water by a stand of black willow, partly shaded
by sycamores. Drawn up in the reeds I could see the
bow of a skiff. Had he known it was there?

"You're making a mistake," I said quietly. "Mordecai
is here. You will never get out of the hills."

He laughed without humor. "Don't be silly! Just drop
that bag and back off."

"Look! Please! My blue dress is in there! Let me
have that, at least! It's the only pretty dress I ever had!"

"All right, get it out and be damned. But hurry! I
haven't time for any more nonsense!"

I opened the bag and thrust my hand in, pulling out
the blue dress and bonnet with my left hand, and the
Doune pistol with my right. I was going to shoot right
through the dress but couldn't stand the thought of
ruining that beautiful gown.

I threw the dress aside, revealing the Doune pistol.

There was a moment of frozen silence; Horst's own
pistol was in his hand, but lowered. There was shock in
his eyes. He stared at me with awful realization. Then I
shot him.

He stood for just an instant, trying to lift his pistol,
but the gun slipped from his fingers into the dust and
he fell, knees first, buckling slowly, and then sprawled
in the dust and leaves. After a moment one of his legs
straightened, the toe digging into the earth.

I walked over to a big sycamore and sat down abruptly,
leaning my head back against the tree.

I was sitting like that when they came down the trail
to the river, Mordecai Sackett and Dorian Chantry.

Dorian came to me and helped me to my feet and
put his arms around me. "It's all right," he said. "Everything is all right."

"I want to go home."

"All right." He folded the blue dress and bonnet and returned them to the bag. Then he picked it up. Together we started away, but Mordecai stopped us.

"Foolish to walk when that skiff's handy. You might as well float down."

"Thank you, Mordecai, for coming."

"Trulove an' Macon, they come too. They're up yonder cleanin' up what's left. We come when needed, cousin. We come when needed." Mordecai glanced at Dorian Chantry and said, "I found a black man in the woods."

"Was he hurt?"

"He'd been shot. Grazed his skull, knocked him out, I guess. When I saw him, there was a dog lyin' beside him, sort of watchin' over him. He's on his feet now, an' will be comin' along directly."

Mordecai glanced again at Dorian, then at Echo. "You sparkin' him?"

I glanced at Dorian, but he blushed. "You might say that," I said. "You might just say that."

"I hope she is," Dorian said. "I'd hate to go back to Uncle Finian and tell him I lost out."

Regal and Ma were settin' on the porch of an evenin' when we came up the trail from the Cove. They were settin' together and Regal stood tall to shake hands and greet Dorian and give me a little squeeze with an arm about my shoulders.

"We missed you, honey. Have a nice trip?"

"Took me longer than expected," I said.

"Come mornin', I'd have been comin' after you. A man stopped by who said he saw you on a steamboat and you seemed to be in some kind of trouble. His name was Ginery Wooster. He said he had passed the word to Mordecai on his way across the mountains."

"We saw Mordecai."

"That's more than I ever did. Come on inside."

We paused a moment on the step, looking off toward Cligman's Dome. The clouds were gathering there. A nighthawk swooped by and Dorian and I turned toward the house.

"See? I told you it was a log cabin!"

# AUTHOR'S NOTE

There should be, within the next few years, at least ten more novels involving members of the Sackett family. These upcoming books will not only close the gap between the novels of the early Sackett generations (SACKETT'S LAND, TO THE FAR BLUE MOUNTAINS, and THE WARRIOR'S PATH) and the novels of the later generations beginning with THE DAYBREAKERS, but will extend the Sackett's story in several new directions. The present novel, RIDE THE RIVER, helps to bridge that gap since Echo Sackett is the aunt of the Sackett brothers William Tell, Orrin, and Tyrel whom we first meet in THE DAYBREAKERS and SACKETT.

The next Sackett novel will be THE SAGA OF JUBAL SACKETT dealing with the area west of the Mississippi, the Great Plains and the Rockies in the years after 1630. At that time this area was the great unknown. Coronado and other Spanish explorers had touched upon it, but their limited explorations were not known to the rest of the world. Even the Indians, who were only beginning to acquire horses, knew little of that vast land in the interior. The distance between streams and known waterholes had restricted their travel until horses were available.

Into this world, teeming with game of every variety, Jubal Sackett travels with one Indian companion seeing it all when it was fresh and new. They hunt buffalo, elk, deer, antelope, bear, and other animals, some of which were believed to have been extinct, all at a time when every step they took was into unknown land.

Later, there will be another story of William Tell Sackett, going back to his earlier years when he first left the Tennessee Mountains to fight in the Civil War. This story will also relate the great romance of his life, or at least the first chapter in it, a romance about which he has told no one, not even his brothers.

# ABOUT LOUIS L'AMOUR

*"I think of myself in the oral tradition—as a troubador, a village taleteller, the man in the shadows of the campfire. That's the way I'd like to be remembered—as a storyteller. A good storyteller."*

It is doubtful that any author could be as at home in the world re-created in his novels as Louis Dearborn L'Amour. Not only could he physically fill the boots of the rugged characters he writes about, but he literally has "walked the land my characters walk." His personal experiences as well as his lifelong devotion to historical research have combined to give Mr. L'Amour the unique knowledge and understanding of the people, events, and challenge of the American frontier which have become the hallmarks of his popularity.

Of French-Irish descent, Mr. L'Amour can trace his own family in North America back to the early 1600s and follow their steady progression westward, "always on the frontier." As a boy growing up in Jamestown, North Dakota, he absorbed all he could about his family's frontier heritage, including the story of his great-grandfather who was scalped by Sioux warriors.

Spurred by an eager curiosity and desire to broaden his horizons, Mr. L'Amour left home at the age of fifteen and enjoyed a wide variety of jobs including seaman, lumberjack, elephant handler, skinner of dead cattle, assessment miner, and officer on tank destroyers during World War II. During his "yondering days" he also circled the world on a freighter, sailed a dhow on the Red Sea, was shipwrecked in the West Indies and stranded in the Mojave Desert. He has won fifty-one of fifty-nine fights as a professional boxer and worked as a journalist and lecturer. A voracious reader and collector of rare books, Mr. L'Amour's personal library of some 10,000 volumes covers a broad range of scholarly disciplines including many personal papers, maps, and diaries of the pioneers.

Mr. L'Amour "wanted to write almost from the time I could walk." After developing a widespread following for his many adventure stories written for the fiction magazines, Mr. L'Amour published his first full-length novel, *Hondo*, in 1953. Mr. L'Amour is now one of the four bestselling living novelists in the world. Every one of his more than 85 novels is constantly in print and every one has sold more than one million copies, giving him more million-copy bestsellers than any other living author. His books have been translated into more than a dozen languages, and more than thirty of his novels and stories have been made into feature films and television movies.

The recipient of many great honors and awards, Mr. L'Amour in 1983 became the first novelist ever to be awarded a Special National Gold Medal by the United States Congress in honor of his life's work. In 1984 he was also awarded the Medal of Freedom by President Ronald Reagan.

Mr. L'Amour lives in Los Angeles with his wife, Kathy, and their two children, Beau and Angelique.